PRA

Jada Sly, Artist & Spy

"Jada Sly: she's **smart**, she's **fun**."
—*School Library Journal*

"**A beginner thriller** with some real gems in it."
—*Kirkus Reviews*

"[A] **fast-paced**, fun novel."
—*School Library Connection*

"Jada [Sly] is a determined young spy-in-training
who would give **an adolescent James Bond**
a run for his money." —*The Bulletin*

"Winston has created a **spunky** character in Jada,
a fashionable artist and independent girl who
isn't afraid to take on a few adults in the search
for the truth." —*Booklist*

ALSO BY SHERRI WINSTON

President of the Whole Fifth Grade
President of the Whole Sixth Grade
President of the Whole Sixth Grade: Girl Code

The Sweetest Sound

JADA SLY

ARTIST & SPY

SHERRI WINSTON

LITTLE, BROWN AND COMPANY
New York Boston

Copyright © 2019 by Sherri Winston
Excerpt from *The Sweetest Sound* copyright © 2017 by Sherri Winston

Cover art copyright © 2019 by Sherri Winston. Cover design by Marcie Lawrence. Cover copyright © 2019 by Hachette Book Group, Inc.

Little, Brown and Company
Hachette Book Group
1290 Avenue of the Americas, New York, NY 10104
Visit us at LBYR.com

Originally published in hardcover and ebook by Little, Brown and Company in May 2019
First Trade Paperback Edition: May 2020

Little, Brown and Company is a division of Hachette Book Group, Inc. The Little, Brown name and logo are trademarks of Hachette Book Group, Inc.

The publisher is not responsible for websites (or their content) that are not owned by the publisher.

The Library of Congress has cataloged the hardcover edition as follows:
Names: Winston, Sherri, author.
Title: Jada Sly, artist & spy / by Sherri Winston.
Description: First edition. | New York ; Boston : Little, Brown and Company, 2019. | Summary: "Jada Sly, artist and spy with a flair for all things French, is on a mission to find her missing mom, who she believes was also a spy"—Provided by publisher.
Identifiers: LCCN 2018028632| ISBN 9780316505369 (hardcover) | ISBN 9780316505352 (ebook) | ISBN 9780316505345
(library edition ebook)
Subjects: | CYAC: Spies—Fiction. | Missing persons—Fiction. | Mothers and daughters—Fiction. | Friendship—Fiction. | Family life—New York (State)—New York—Fiction. | New York (N.Y.)—Fiction.
Classification: LCC PZ7.W7536 Jad 2019 | DDC [Fic]—dc23
LC record available at https://lccn.loc.gov/2018028632

ISBNs: 978-0-316-50533-8 (pbk.), 978-0-316-50535-2 (ebook)

PRINTED IN CHINA

APS

10 9 8 7 6 5

To my sister Jennifer ... girl, you
never gave up on my crazy idea that
one day I would illustrate a book.
It's just me and you.

CHAPTER 1

Our Air France direct flight from Bordeaux to New York City trembled and shook.

Exhaust thundered from the engines. Plumes of fire ate away the sides of the plane. Would I be able to save everyone? Or were we doomed?

Heart hammering, I gripped my sketchbook, drawing fast to capture the faces of enemy agents determined to take over our plane.

Smoke from the fiery aircraft burned my eyes and nose. The enemies swarmed the plane. Something had to be done.

My spy training kicked in.

This was what I'd prepared for.

Slow, steady breaths. In-out-in-out. Just like my ballet teacher, Madame Geneviève, had taught me.

Then I switched from ballet techniques to martial arts. My muscles strained. Knee bent; foot tucked under my butt—I was ready to strike.

The enemies began to surround me. Muscles tight as drums. Teeth gritted. And then—

"Mademoiselle, are you feeling unwell?" A French accent rose above the chaos.

It was the flight attendant hovering at the end of our aisle. She looked down at Cécile, my father's museum colleague. "Madame, is the young lady going to be all right?"

The burning trails of engine smoke evaporated.

The charred airplane returned to normal.

No enemies dashed down the aisle or lunged for my journal of top-secret sketches, mementos, and the faces of would-be assassins. And none of the passengers cried for help or even looked distressed.

Cécile reached over and squeezed my hand. She assured the flight attendant that I was *très bien.*

After a long moment, the flight attendant left us.

I chewed on my lip, lowered my foot, and drew a deep breath.

"You are going to be just fine, *ma chérie*," Cécile said. "This is only your third flight since..."

Her voice faltered. She was going to say *since the accident*.

"I *am* fine," I said, resolutely. Papa used to say I was the most "resolute" young lady he'd ever known. *Resolute*, meaning "determined." Back then, he meant it as a compliment. Now, well, a lot had changed.

My name is Sly. Jada Sly. I am an artist. And I am a SPY! One of my talents is remembering faces. I love to draw and observe the shapes and curves that make people's faces. Being a great observer—and artist—is going to help me become the best international spy one day.

I was in the midst of the greatest mission I'd probably ever have—one that could change my life forever.

Understand, I wasn't some superbrilliant kid genius with a million gadgets who belonged to a secret agency that employed other superbrilliant young geniuses—the kinds of kids you read about in made-up stories.

3

I was simply me. A girl who had grown up playing spy games, solving puzzles, and digging up buried secrets. Not to mention my knack for memorizing the angles of a person's face and form. As I said, I was also an artist. Honestly, it was in my blood.

The airplane glided above puffy white clouds, and I continued to keep a watchful eye. I needed my nerves calm and my focus steady.

On the seat between Cécile and me sat my pet bunny, Josephine Baker. She had been sleeping in her cage. Fat and cuddly. Larger than most bunny rabbits, with ivory-and-caramel-colored fur and large droopy ears. She was a highly skilled operative, capable of decoding complex calculations, but she was also just so furry that stroking her calmed my nerves. Mostly that second part, actually.

I loved dreaming up spy scenarios and practicing missions with a few of my friends back home in Bordeaux. Sometimes I got really caught up in my imagination.

Lately, though, it seemed the scenarios I dreamed up were feeling more and more real. Too real. Papa said I was having something called a panic attack.

He said it was normal, given what all our family had been through.

But I didn't want the panic attacks to be my new normal.

My reflection in the plane's window made me smile. I couldn't help touching my hair again. I used to wear ponytails. Now it was cut in a daring and bold style—with bangs that swept across my cheek and covered one eye.

Papa had laughed when I'd returned from the salon looking brand-new. Then he'd hugged me so tight I thought my lungs would explode.

He was already in New York. He'd left a few weeks earlier in preparation for the reopening of our family's museum, the Sly. He was going to be the new director.

Cécile was born in Bordeaux. She worked with my dad in France. When he decided to move back to New York, she agreed to come, too. I had stayed behind because of a summer trip with my classmates. Now I was arriving weeks after the American schools had begun. I hadn't been to school in the United States since prekindergarten. It was going to be strange feeling like a foreigner in my own country.

"*Chérie*," she said, her French accent a joyous mixture of syllables, "what are you thinking about with such intensity? I can practically feel your imaginative brain working."

I reached across to playfully nudge her.

As much as I loved Cécile, and Papa, I had to remind myself that they were keeping secrets from me, too.

Grown-ups always think they should be the ones with secrets. They believe in honesty only when it benefits them. I tell you, if young people weren't natural-born spies, we'd never find out anything. Allow me to give an example:

I was 100 percent positive Mama had not worked as a Foreign Service Officer at the US embassy while we'd been living in Bordeaux. That was what she told everyone. I knew better. She had to be a real-life, honest-to-goodness spy.

Of course, no one, especially Papa, would confirm it.

Six months earlier, Mama was flying a plane. It crashed somewhere over the Atlantic Ocean. (The very ocean we were now flying over!) No bodies were ever found.

Doesn't that sound suspicious? It did to me. Like the kind of thing that could happen only if my mother were a spy. I wonder if learning to fly a plane was something Mama did to become a spy. Hmm...I'll have to put it on my list of things to learn, just in case.

Mama was the one who played all sorts of spy games with me. She knew I liked hiding in her big double closet, looking for classified information. Like birthday presents meant for me!

One year, for Christmas, all my gifts were hidden. I had to use tracking coordinates to find them.

We used to watch old spy movies. She thought my love of espionage was wonderful. Papa preferred quizzing me on art and art history. He was always asking me to look at my surroundings and tell him what famous painter came to mind.

He had changed since the accident. When I told him about my belief that Mama had not died in the crash, he wanted me to see a psychologist.

But what I needed—desperately—was answers.

I was running out of time.

My parents had been the perfect couple. Sure, they didn't do a lot of things together. In fact, in the year before the accident, Papa and I were spending more and more time together, while Mama was spending more and more time away.

I'd been angry at her about that.

Not now. Because surely, she had been gone because of secret missions.

Thanks to the skills she taught me, I had discovered another important secret. It was about Papa and Cécile.

In the past few months, I'd begun to notice how he looked at her and blushed when she looked at him, how he'd started wearing clean cardigans to work rather than the messy ones with rips and stains.

I needed answers because, way deep in my soul, I knew Mama wasn't dead. She was merely in hiding to protect Papa and me. She had been in danger, and maybe we were, too. I just knew it. I had this feeling.

More than a feeling—I had proof.

The only other flights I'd taken since she disappeared had been to New York City for her memorial and back to Bordeaux. Mama, whose mother was African American and father was Egyptian, grew up in the city. Mama loved some art—not the way Papa got all gooey-eyed about a painting, but she knew what she liked. Edgar Degas's drawings and paintings of ballet dancers were her favorites.

I'd had a tiny replica of Edgar Degas's famous *Little Dancer* sculpture. At the grave site the day of Mama's memorial, I left the figurine behind.

A few days after Papa and I returned to Bordeaux, I awoke in the middle of the night. I had a strange feeling, like someone had been in my room. The faint smell of Mama's favorite fragrance, Coco Chanel, lingered around me.

And there on the nightstand stood the figurine.

Of course, Papa insisted the next day that I must have brought it back with me. He thought it made more sense to believe that I'd somehow forgot and left a statuette on my own nightstand—even though it was supposed to be thousands of miles away in a cemetery!

I wanted to argue with him about it.

I needed someone to believe me.

My mother was alive.

And I was going to find her.

CHAPTER 2

Another thing Mama and I used to do was to go people-watching at the park or somewhere with lots of people.

Cécile and I walked briskly through the airport. I glanced about as I went. I liked field-testing my techniques whenever possible. I did have a knack for recognizing faces.

It didn't take long before I spotted a tall man with a rectangular face and long arms. Was he speaking into his jacket?

This is it, I thought.

Fearing karate or judo or tae kwon do might be our only salvation, I prepared for battle. My French martial arts teacher, Master Chin-d' Maitre, said what I lacked in technique I more than made up for with spirit.

My body was coiled, ready for action. I felt strong but chic in my polka-dotted dress and matching handbag.

Just as I was about to strike, however, the man nodded toward Cécile. That was when I saw it—a Bluetooth earpiece in his ear. He wasn't an enemy agent keeping an eye on us. Just some businessman barking instructions to his secretary, no doubt.

I exhaled, remaining vigilant. I seriously couldn't shake the feeling that someone was watching me.

We retrieved our bags and walked to the taxi stand. September sunshine poured over us with warmth despite the cool breeze.

Cécile chatted easily with a man in the taxi line. However, I felt a definite prickle on the back of my neck. It wasn't the September breeze. My head remained on a constant swivel. Were we being followed? One never knew!

In the tall windows of the terminal I caught a

glimpse of someone. A person who was staring right at us. A woman.

Mama?

As the thought slammed into my brain, I felt a tug on my arm—then a hard yank!

"Hey there, now!" yelled Cécile.

A faceless figure hidden beneath a hoodie. Long, athletic build. He shoved me while gripping the strap of the bag on my arm. Thin arms with a body shaped like a long flat eraser.

Yanking my bag back, I kicked out my foot as though in preparation for a grand jeté. But rather than leaping, I flicked my foot upward. The kick landed solidly above his kneecap. He buck-led long enough for the man who'd been talking to Cécile to turn and grab his sleeve. But the thief shoved him before he finally tore free and raced away.

"My word!" Cécile was saying.

The police rushed over. People started talking all at once, asking if I was okay. I wasn't paying much attention.

My eyes were searching the tall windows of the

terminal. But the late-afternoon sunlight had turned them into mirrors. The woman was gone.

Had it really been Mama?

She was the right height. The hair had been the same, too—short and dark and smooth.

"Miss, are you all right?" The police officer's eyes were filled with concern.

"Yes, yes," I said. "I'm fine. Really!"

The grown-ups needed to discuss it some more, but I wanted to get out of there. I was tired of all these strangers staring at me or patting me on the shoulder.

What if he wasn't just some random thief?

Even as the thought raced through my brain, Cécile was giving me a gentle push into the taxi. Soon as my bottom hit the seat, we were whisked away from John F. Kennedy Airport toward the city.

"I'm so sorry that happened to you, sweetie," she was saying. Her arm draped protectively over me. She gave my shoulder a squeeze.

The cab driver stopped at the next red light and looked over the seat. He said, "Hey, young lady, was that your first mugging?" He grinned, showing tobacco-stained teeth.

I sat as straight and tall as I could. I said, "Well, as a matter of fact, it was."

Cécile gave my shoulder another squeeze. The cabbie said, "Welcome to New York, ladies!"

Indeed.

CHAPTER 3

As we rode into town, the world around me exploded with sights and smells and sounds. Noise from a thousand yellow taxis honking. Planes roaring overhead leaving curly gray tails. Leafy green streets sprouting impossibly tall buildings. And a million dark corners and hidden alleyways.

Normally, such a thing would be artistic inspiration. Spy possibilities, too.

But I was having trouble concentrating.

Had Mama been at the airport?

What about the thief? Was it truly some random mugging?

Or was there more to it?

The Degas replica statuette weighed down the corner of my sweater pocket.

My thoughts drifted to the clue hidden away in my bag. The one and only clue I had to finding Mama. I chewed on my lip.

Josephine Baker stirred in her cage.

The real Josephine Baker didn't have whiskers or a cute pink nose. She did, however, have other wonderful qualities, such as being a legendary black female entertainer who captured the heart of Paris with her music, while also spying for the French Resistance.

I hoped to capture her style and mystique with my dress, touched off with my red scarf and red cashmere cardigan. Very French. Thinking of my outfit made me smile. Good fashion sense always soothed me.

Before long we were rolling to a stop in front of my new home on the Upper West Side. Even though Bordeaux—where I'd spent the past five years of my life with my parents—would always be home to me, the familiar sight of the Sly family brownstone brought a smile to my lips.

Grandmother Sly had lived here for decades. Now she lived at the Dakota, one of those fancy New York City buildings with its own name. Papa said people like Grandmother Sly loved the Dakota because it showed off their wealth and status to the world without them having to do anything as vulgar as talk about money. Whatever that meant.

Since the Slys had owned this brownstone—as well as several others—for generations, my grandmother felt it only made sense that Papa and I live here now.

"The Slys have lived in this building since 1922," Grandmother Sly always said to Papa during her long-distance calls while we were in Bordeaux.

Grandmother was quite proud of her husband's family legacy. She said managing to own property in America during the 1920s was a coup for African Americans. Grandpa's grandfather was a daring businessman who acquired lots of money and land despite being the son of former slaves.

Grandmother took being a Sly very seriously. Mama once told me, "Being a Sly comes with a lot of responsibilities—ones Eleanor takes seriously." I didn't know quite what that meant, either, but Grandmother Sly was all about her business.

She was also all about everyone else's.

Which was why my heart sank into my soft leather ballet flats when I walked through the foyer and saw her standing in the living room. *Gulp!*

"Well, don't just stand there gawking, child. Come give your dear grandmother a hug," she said.

"Grandmother Sly!" I forced my voice into a cheery tone. I went over and gave her a hug. She did that thing adults do when they haven't seen you in a while, remarking on my height, how I'd grown, and so on.

"Jada! What have you done to your hair?" she said, swatting away at the bangs artfully draped over my eye.

I pulled back, saying I liked my new hairstyle. A spy was all about mystique.

"Mrs. Sly, so very good to see you," Cécile said, giving my grandmother a French welcome—a double air-kiss.

The sound of shuffling interrupted us.

Papa stood in the narrow hallway, body half turned as if he couldn't decide if he was going left or right, backward or forward. A pen was clenched in his teeth while pencils speared his curly hair at odd angles. Papa was like that. A bit of a nutty professor type.

When he finally looked up and saw Cécile, the first thing he did was try to fix his hair, which only caused a rain shower of pencils diving to the floor.

He tore himself away from staring at Cécile and looked in my direction, grinning wide.

"Who is there? Why, I do not recognize this tall, sophisticated, and fashionable young lady."

Oh, he could be so charming.

"Papa!" I remained poised—in spirit, at least—as I raced toward him.

Papa dropped his folders and papers onto the floor, swept me up, and spun me around.

"Ahh, *ma petite lapine*!" he said. "Ooph! You have grown so much."

I reminded him that I was way too mature to be twirled about.

"For heaven's sake, Benjamin, put her down. She's a young lady now, not a baby," said Grandmother Sly, adding, "Did you know about this...this hairstyle?"

Papa ignored her. He pressed his nose to mine.

His expression changed to I'm-trying-to-look-serious-but-I'm-really-not. He said, "Have you kept up your art studies over the summer?"

"Papa—"

"Benjamin Elijah Sly, do not ignore me," said Grandmother.

He put me down. But he kept his professor face on with his hands on his hips. Oh, for goodness' sake. Grown-ups really could be too much.

I knew the game he wanted to play. It was easier to just go along with it.

"So tell me, who painted *The Lady in Gold*?"

"Gustav Klimt," I said, forcing a smile. "Of course, the actual name is *Portrait of Adele Bloch-Bauer I*."

"Very good!" he said with a grin.

Cécile cleared her throat and took that opportunity to announce that I'd practically been mugged at the airport.

I'd almost forgotten the bizarre incident.

"I'm fine," I said, seeing the shocked look on Papa's face. I glanced over at Cécile, who announced she was going to make tea. Traitor! Now I was stuck between Papa's bewildered expression and Grandmother Sly and her judgy eyebrows.

Grandmother Sly's gaze shifted between Papa and me, then her tone cracked like a whip. "Benjamin! How could you let a thing like this happen?"

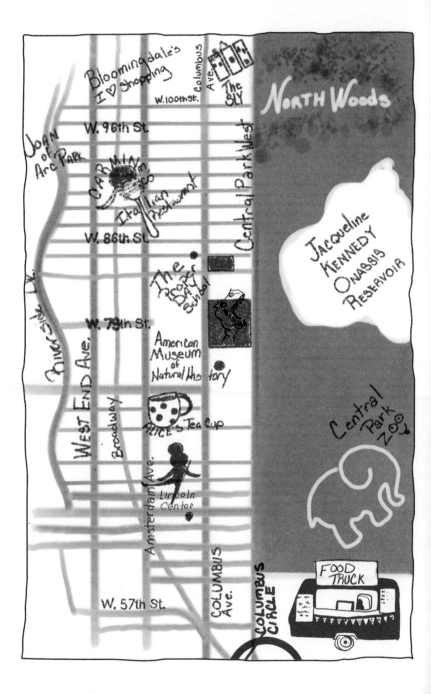

CHAPTER 4

"Oh, hello, Mother. I didn't hear you come in." He said it as though he was only now realizing she was in the room. Grandmother Sly's presence was always known.

She cast a glance at him. Sleek in her emerald-green suit, with shoes so pointy they could be considered lethal weapons, my grandmother arched one delicately drawn eyebrow.

"Benjamin! What on earth is to be done about my granddaughter's safety?" she demanded.

"Mother, she's home safe," he said before turning to me. "Jada, are you sure you're all right?"

"I'm fine, Papa, really."

He turned back to Grandmother Sly. "Case closed," he said.

She made a disgusted sound, and Cécile reappeared with a tea tray, offering my grandmother a cup.

Papa looked at Grandmother Sly once again, now with narrowed eyes.

"Mother, why exactly are you here?"

"Now, is that any way to greet the woman who gave you life?" she said. Whenever Grandmother mentioned how she'd given Papa life, I cringed. I mean, really, that was not something I needed to hear. Cécile was trying not to laugh.

"Of course, hello, Mother." He gave her a peck on the cheek and a quick hug. Then he stepped back. "Seriously, Mother, to what do we owe the pleasure of your company?"

"I wanted to greet my granddaughter, of course. As well as let her know her ballet classes are all set."

Papa looked a little annoyed, but he smiled. "Yes, of course. And thank you again, Mother, for helping me set up a dance demonstration at the museum for our reopening in a few weeks."

My grandmother flicked a glance, as if to say *I am fabulous and all-knowing, of course!* Even though her habit of sticking her nose in our business could be annoying, I was glad she had butted in. The Belyakov School was where Mama had studied dance while she was in college. My lessons had started there when I was three.

"Excuse me, I'd like to go to my room," I said, picking up Josephine's cage.

"Please wash your hands after handling that creature," my dear grandmother called behind me. "I'm taking you and Cécile out to dinner to celebrate your return!"

Pause.

"You're welcome to come, too, Benjamin," she said.

Even with my back turned and my face pointing in the opposite direction, when Papa said, "Gee, thank you, Mother," I could almost hear the sound of her brows being raised yet again. I smothered a laugh and went to my room.

My gaze swept around my new bedroom and

took in the pale pink walls, a pearly off-white carpet, and the reproductions of some of my favorite famous artworks. It was beautiful. If I hadn't been positive we'd be moving back to Bordeaux soon—with Mama—it would have been a room I could fall in love with.

I began unpacking my clothes, shoes, and matching bags. French girls needed an abundance of black-and-white-striped tops or plain white ones. So did American girls wanting to be stylish among their French friends. I was certain striped tees were required by law passed down from Marie Antoinette.

When I finished putting away my things, a stray beam of sunlight streaked one pale pink wall. A tiny bit of *parfum* in Mama's almost empty Coco Chanel bottle caught the light and broke it into hundreds of diamond shapes, like a prism. The kaleidoscope pattern refracted against the wall looked exactly like a Zentangle drawing.

The last day before Mama left, we'd lain across the king-sized bed in her bedroom, coloring. She loved coloring books filled with doodles and shapes. She liked taking them on her trips, so we began working on a picture together before she left. She said having it would make her feel like we were still coloring together.

With only Josephine as a witness, I reached inside my bag and removed a classic red quilted Chanel purse with a gold-chain strap.

When I heard of Mama's accident, I wanted to hold on to everything that was hers. Papa didn't allow it, but he did let me keep the purse. Once I had a chance to look through it, I was shocked.

Inside was a postcard with a reproduction of Degas's *Three Dancers in Red Costume*. It had been one of Mama's favorite paintings, and she told me it reminded her of me. After the accident, I'd thought a lot about that day, and I remembered something:

While we were coloring that last day, she received a phone call. She took one of the Degas postcards we'd bought earlier in the day from her bag to write a note.

After that she grew fidgety and kept checking the window for her taxi. We went downstairs to the living room. Papa called her into the kitchen to talk. When she came out, it looked like she wanted to cry. He stood in the doorway, hands in his pockets, pain in his eyes.

I tried asking what was wrong, but the taxi honked. Mama brushed a kiss across my head, looked at Papa, then was gone.

Weeks later, after the plane crash, I went through her purse.

That was when I first saw the postcard with the note scrawled on the back. It had to mean something.

She'd written *Charles* and circled *21*.

Charles?

Now six months had passed. I'd waited patiently for a chance to come back to New York City. One clue. A name and a number. Not a lot, but all I had to work with.

I had an idea who Charles was. But I needed to find him.

CHAPTER 5

We sat at an outdoor table at an Italian café.

It was early evening. Purples and grays smeared the sky. I leaned my art journal against the table. Working quickly, I tried to capture the feel of all the movement—people walking purposefully in one direction while others moved slowly in the opposite direction.

New York City was so busy and alive with movement and sound. In some ways it reminded me of the times I'd visited Paris with Papa. He often worked with museums there, too.

Sitting at a Paris café always made me feel like I

was in a Henri Matisse painting with beautiful, colorful people all around.

New York City, on the other hand, was a total Kandinsky. Wassily Kandinsky was a Russian painter. A genius! He did a lot of cool abstract paintings—usually full of color, shapes, zigs, and zags. Lots of energy, lots of *zing*—like New York!

"Oh, Jada, it is so good to have you back home," said Grandmother Sly for the third time since we'd sat down. She reached over and squeezed my cheeks.

"Mother, you're going to bruise her face," Papa said. He gave me a look that said *Please excuse your grandmother*.

When he looked at Cécile, his cheeks went pink, and I tried really hard not to roll my eyes. I had to nip this—whatever it was—in the bud before it got any worse.

"I'm just so grateful to have my granddaughter home," she said.

"Mother," Papa repeated, drawing out the word, not hiding his annoyance.

Cécile and I laughed. Grandmother was so over-the-top.

She reached over again, but instead of pinching my cheeks, she stroked my face. She was acting as though I'd been kidnapped rather than living in a farmhouse in France.

Grandmother Sly sighed.

"I can live with the hair," she said. "It makes you look mysterious. A young lady deserves a little mystery."

I touched her hand. She was strong, alert, and fierce. Her gray eyes were more silvery than mine. Her cheekbones sharp as daggers.

Still, when she looked at me, I knew she loved me, and I loved her, too. The thought brought an unexpected lump to my throat.

"Mom," Papa said, more gently than his earlier wail, "I know how much you love Jada—"

"Love you both!" she said urgently.

"We love you, too," he said.

She sniffed. But when she spoke again, it was with her usual huff.

"Then why do I have to practically kidnap you for dinner?" she said dryly. She was back. Papa did another one of his eye rolls.

Papa and Grandmother Sly were constantly bickering. Not really arguing, but she didn't always remember he wasn't twelve years old anymore. And when he was around her, he didn't seem to remember, either.

It was kind of funny to see him treated like the child for a change. I was still smiling when I first noticed a medium-sized, boxy truck.

I simply must tell you that the first thing that popped into my mind was *What if that truck is being driven by masterminds of some criminal conspiracy?* I could have sworn there was a man on top of the truck. Stealthy and slick.

The truck seemed unsteady. The man on top was crouched, arms out, muscles tight. Like Spider-Man. Only this looked more like the Marvel villain Venom, gleaming black against the nighttime sky.

The truck's lights were on. Their shape in the truck's wide-nosed grille looked like malevolent eyes. (If you read as much spy fiction and as many comic books as I do, you need to know what *malevolent* means. Trust me!)

Up ahead, beyond Cécile's shoulder, the truck started to career. The figure on top stayed poised.

My heart fluttered in my chest. Only, this time,

instead of foreign agents, it was an out-of-control truck destined to crash into the diners, leaving us all in a smoldering heap.

The tiny white lights surrounding the patio reflected and bounced off Cécile's glittering jewelry.

By now I had stopped drawing. I set aside my pen, curled my fingers into fists. Calmly as I could, I blew in and out. I opened and closed my fingers and eyes.

A horn blared.

Another horn honked.

I couldn't just sit there, waiting to be plowed down.

Just as I was about to sweep everyone away from the oncoming truck's path, another loud blare caused me to shriek.

"Jada!" Papa said.

Breath felt ragged in my chest. I blinked.

"Jada?" Papa's voice was softer now.

"Yes, Papa, I'm fine. The...the horn startled me, that's all," I said.

One final look at the truck, and I swallowed the lump in my throat. Venom turned out to be a black plastic figure. Of a giant bug. The truck had not exactly careened. More like swerved to avoid another car.

After a few more moments passed, Papa said, "Okay...if that is all..."

Grandmother Sly placed the back of her hand to my forehead, checking for a fever. No matter what your problem was, my grandmother always believed it started with a fever.

"She feels feverish, son," she said.

I groaned.

"Mother, that horn could've scared anyone," Papa said. Although, when I looked at him, I saw even he didn't completely believe himself.

A shiver ran through me. Was my mind playing tricks on me again?

I tried to lose myself between the pages of my journal. The truck was real. But the picture in my brain—the one showing bad guys and out-of-control trucks—was not real.

The last thing I needed was for Papa to become more concerned.

I remembered how worried he was after Mama's accident, and that he'd called my pediatrician.

Dr. Yamato told him it was common for children

suffering with a loss to believe their loved one was still alive.

"Give her some time," Dr. Yamato had urged. Then he told my papa that if I continued to "struggle with reality," I should see someone.

By "someone," he meant a therapist for kids. Papa was always giving me secret glances to determine whether I was feeling okay.

Dinner was served. I hadn't realized how hungry I was. The three grown-ups talked about the upcoming exhibit being held in a few weeks. The Sly had been closed for months. Papa called it a "soft opening." Meaning that there would be a small celebration, with a much bigger event planned for the grand opening.

"I still can't believe I managed to find a shoe dating all the way back forty thousand years," Papa said.

He had been collecting ancient shoes from all over the world since before I was born. He said it was another way to study cultural history.

Cécile nodded at him as if to say forty-thousand-year-old shoes were the most important discovery since the sun or the iPhone.

I went back to my sketch journal, trying to hide

my laughter. For a while, I'd been trying to re-create the shapes and colors of the airport attacker. He was fast. And lean. And strong. But there was something about him, the way he moved, that felt—off. I couldn't quite figure it out.

With a sigh, I switched to working on a map of the Upper West Side. People who'd never been there usually couldn't imagine how long the island of Manhattan was. I had friends in Bordeaux who thought all of New York City was the size of Times Square. That's only one neighborhood!

The Upper West Side was the neighborhood between Central Park and the Hudson River. When I was little, I loved hanging out at the Sly almost as much as I did Central Park, which was right across the street from the museum.

The waiter brought the check. Grandmother and Papa tugged on it until it tore in half, and exchanged blaming glares with each other.

Grandmother Sly took that as a victory and waved at a passing waiter.

Papa was still shaking his head when his phone buzzed.

"What's wrong?" I said. His eyes had gone

completely wide. Excitement and alarm tag-teamed my pulse. I couldn't help hoping every beep, buzz, or jingle of the phone might somehow come with a message from Mama.

But what he said next was shocking in a whole other way.

"We must go now. It's the alarm company. Some-one has broken into the Sly!"

CHAPTER 6

Two police cars with their roof lights flashing sat outside the Sly.

It had been two years since I'd been at the museum. When we came to New York for Mama's memorial, I wasn't interested in visiting.

Now, seeing it in the red-and-blue glare of police lights felt unsettling.

The police at first made us all wait outside until they secured the perimeter—police language for walking around the building looking for any signs of bad guys.

Afterward, Papa went inside with them, but the rest of us were asked to wait on the steps outside.

"I can't take waiting out here," I said suddenly. "I'm going in!"

Cécile reached for me, and I heard Grandmother say, "No, you will not!"

I pushed through the doors before either could stop me. Immediately, I was plunged into shadowy darkness. My hand swept the wall where the switch was located.

I flipped it.

Nothing happened.

Removing my phone from my bag, I turned on the flashlight and shined it around the entryway. Dust fluttered in the light's beam.

"Papa?" I called softly. I tried several other light switches, but none resulted in more light.

"Jada Marie Sly!"

"Grandmother—"

"Don't you 'Grandmother' me, child. You practically gave me a heart attack, rushing in here like that!"

From the *clickity-clack* of high heels, I knew Cécile had joined us as well. The three of us stood motionless in the darkness. I strained to see into the front room, which I knew to be the children's parlor.

My heart was thudding. I stared in the direction of the basement doors, half expecting anything from a robber to Frankenstein's monster. Inky shapes and angles filled the entryway, which was lit by my phone, streetlights, and the moon.

Was my imagination running away with me again? Or was a door down the hall beginning to open?

I turned my head to see if Cécile had noticed the same thing, but she was preoccupied with her own phone. Trying to text Papa. I drew a deep breath.

When I looked back at the door, it was unmistakable. The door was definitely opening.

Something had to be done, so I lunged forward.

"Jada, stop!" hissed Grandmother Sly. I was too quick.

Just as I pushed the door, a voice from the other side said, "OW!"

At that moment, the lights came on, flooding the lower level. Voices rose from down a separate set of stairs. Papa and the police officers.

I turned to find a tall, thin man wearing a black turtleneck and black slacks, blond hair swept across his forehead. He was scowling down at me.

"You almost took off my finger trying to slam that door closed," he said.

"All clear," Papa was calling from a hallway in the third of the three buildings that made up the Sly. He saw the man looking down at me and rushed over.

All right, stranger. You're toast!

However, rather than confronting the stranger with the oblong head and diamond-shaped face, or even telling the police to take him away, Papa's face broke into a big smile.

"Allister! Good to see you. I see you've met my daughter, Jada?" he asked.

"Yes," said this Allister person. He barely tried to hide the snarl in his voice.

"Allister Highborne, meet Jada Sly," Papa continued. His voice got this upbeat, loud tone whenever he was with his work people. He was grinning, hoping we'd like each other. "He's my assistant."

One look at Mr. Highborne, and I knew that wasn't going to happen.

He extended a pale bony hand. His nose was long and angular like a ski slope, and he tilted it upward. Very snobby.

While we were shaking hands, Papa asked, "Allister, when did you get here?"

He held up his phone. "I came soon as I got the text. I must've gotten here just before you and the police. I was looking around, but I didn't see anything—or anyone."

Papa nodded. "Of course."

Papa may have bought his story, but I wasn't sure. I stood staring at the man's rectangular features. Something wasn't quite right about him. I could feel it.

Apparently, Grandmother Sly and Cécile already knew Mr. High-and-Mighty Highborne. When I looked at him again, I caught him glaring at me, but I remained cool.

The police did another walk-through, but by then it was clear no one else was in the building. It was getting late, and Papa promised to let me come back on Monday after school.

School!

I'd almost forgotten.

We were outside in the cool air. Papa decided it was best we take a taxi. We all waited while he hailed a cab for Grandmother, who had farther to travel. Papa, Cécile, and Mr. Highborne chatted while we waited for another taxi to come along.

Papa began telling Mr. Highborne about the incident with the mugger at the airport.

"Cécile says my girl gave that guy one heck of a kick," Papa said, grinning.

When I looked at Mr. Highborne, he wasn't smiling.

He was staring right at my red leather-bound art journal with the Sly Museum logo embossed on the cover.

Finally, he looked up and asked, "Where did you get that?"

I drew a deep breath. We *were* standing on the steps of the Sly, the place with the same name that was printed on the cover.

"It came from the museum," I said as politely as I could.

"Did you get it from the museum this afternoon?"

"How do you know I haven't had it for years?" I asked with my hands on my hips.

Papa and Cécile were busy talking about shoes again. Maybe dinosaurs who wore shoes. I wasn't sure.

Mr. Highborne had moved closer to me than I liked. Keeping his eyes on the journal, he said, "This design is fairly new. They haven't been made available to the public yet."

I shrugged, then a memory came to me.

"Mama sent it to me," I said, remembering the phone call she made to me from right here at the Sly. "It was the last time I spoke with her."

Papa called my name and snapped me out of the memory.

"Jada, our ride is here," he said. "Good seeing you tonight, Allister. Thank you for being here."

Before I could walk away, Mr. Highborne said, "Well, I'm glad you had that chance to talk to her. I met your mom. She was a great person—"

"Yes, she was," I said, not wanting to hear this strange man talk about Mama any longer. Still, I couldn't deny that his eyes looked sincere. And maybe a little sad.

I climbed into the taxi. As we drove off, I looked out the window. My neck craned to see Mr. Highborne, who was still standing in the same spot. Staring at the taxi.

I clutched the art journal against me, wondering if I'd ever be able to make everything all right again.

CHAPTER 7

I'm happy to report that after the shocking events of Friday, the rest of the weekend was quiet. However, happiness was in short supply. I was being forced into a gray, white, and red plaid jumper with a white blouse that had a rounded collar. Rounded!

I did what I could, adding my customary red scarf and matching cashmere sweater. I even wore my extra-long white socks with pink and red cat faces. And black Mary Janes, too.

Grandmother Sly, a woman of style, once told me

there was no problem so great that a good pair of Mary Janes couldn't fix it. Glimpsing myself in the darkened shop windows, I knew expecting shoes to overcome the tragedy of this school uniform was too much to ask.

"How do I look?" I asked Papa. We walked along with other people who weren't forced to wear plaid wool. I felt so alone.

"You look like an American private school student," he said.

Sigh. Wearing a uniform meant saying *au revoir* to my panache.

"I look like a fashion failure," I groaned.

This time he laughed aloud. His laughter made me laugh, even though, truly, gray, white, and red plaid was no laughing matter.

Then he paused, catching a glance at himself in a window. He asked, "How do *I* look?"

Papa stood about six feet tall. His curly black hair was almost always unruly.

However, looking at him, I realized he'd combed his hair until it was neat. Instead of his normal ill-fitting suit, he wore a bright print sweater under his suit jacket.

I gave him a pat on the arm. "Papa, you look delightful. I love the colorful sweater!"

He beamed.

"Cécile helped me pick it out. She said I was making myself look too old," he said, smiling shyly. I tried not to groan. Now she was picking out his clothes? *Oh, Cécile!*

We chatted as we walked. By the time we'd descended the steps into the subway station and swiped our MetroCards, I felt like I could tell him anything—like I used to before he started worrying about me.

It gave me an idea. I'd been thinking about my one clue—*Charles* and *21* scrawled on the Degas postcard.

The only Charles I'd ever heard of was a man who'd worked with Mama right here in New York City. I'd met him a few times in her office building on the twenty-first floor. I remembered the floor because it was such a big deal for me to push the button.

Even so, I didn't know his last name or the name of the building.

What if I just asked Papa the name of the building? It was only natural I'd be thinking about Mama now that I was back in New York City, right?

However, before I could ask, I got a weird, skittish feeling on my neck. I turned slowly just in time to see a small man with a squarish head beneath a baseball cap. When he saw me watching, he quickly turned away.

Had he been staring at us?

"What were you asking me?" Papa said, cutting into my observations.

"Yes, I mean, what?" I answered, distracted.

"You were about to say something," he said, turning in the direction of my gaze.

I took a breath, held it in, and slowly exhaled.

"Papa, do you remember when Mama worked in the city? What was that building called where she worked?"

At first, he looked surprised. Then he looked concerned.

"Why, Jada Marie? Why do you want to know?"

This was where I had to be very careful. Ever since Mama's disappearance, Papa had had little patience for my "spy games." Well, he called it games. I called it training. Still, the last time he caught me training, he wasn't happy. I was going through his suit coat pockets. Not for anything special, just as part of my training.

"Papa, I've been thinking about her. Can I help it, being back here?"

He sighed. "As long as you aren't returning to your snooping, I guess. Your mother worked in Lower Manhattan near the Financial District. The Braniff Bank Building, on the twenty-first floor. She worked for that delightful old man." He paused, thinking. Then he snapped his fingers.

"Tillerson. Charles Tillerson! He used to like to do magic tricks and pull quarters out of your ears. Do you remember how much fun we used to have going down there for lunch? There were so many..."

He kept on talking, even after our train screeched away from the platform. But my heart leapt with excitement. I'd been going nuts trying to figure this out for months, and just like that—*snap*—he told me everything.

Almost everything.

Now I had to figure out why Mama wrote that name down in the first place.

The Proper Day School of the Arts.

It sat across the street from the park at Eighty-Fourth Street and Central Park West.

Once we entered the building, I found myself swimming in a sea of plaid. There were jumpers, skirts, and even pants on a few girls. Papa must've been reading the desperate plea for help in my eyes.

He touched my shoulder and assured me, "You'll be fine."

I most certainly would not.

C'est la vie! I would have to make the best of it.

I put on my cheeriest smile and said good-bye. While Papa rushed off to catch the train, I was told that someone would come get me soon.

While I waited, I couldn't help thinking about the guy in the baseball cap. On the subway platform. Sure, New York was crowded and people probably got stared at all the time. Still, he *had* been staring. And he *did* look away when I caught him.

Why?

"So you won't get lost on your first day," said a voice.

The voice startled me.

Even so, my superior self-defense training led me to instantly drop into a shallow standing squat. My weight was evenly distributed over my legs and feet.

I was face-to-face with an African American girl my same age. She was also tall like me. She peered at me. I peered back.

Hmm…

A questioning expression filled her eyes. A second ticked by and then she was standing in a shallow squat position as well.

"Who are you?" I asked. We were circling each other.

"I'm Brooklyn. Everybody calls me Brooklyn from Harlem, because, you know, my name is Brooklyn and I live in Harlem." She said it with a casual shrug. She wore glasses with red plastic frames. Her Afro was a perfectly round crown.

However, behind the glasses her eyes were sharp; her karate technique impressive.

"I'm Sly, Jada Sly," I said. "From France. But I'm

American. Everyone calls me Jada. Well, because it is my name, of course."

Then she said, "Can we stop circling each other now? We cool?"

"Cool," I said. "You just surprised me before."

We both picked up our backpacks, which we'd dropped to the floor.

"I heard you say 'why.' I thought you were asking why you needed a student guide," she said. Now we were walking and talking. Brooklyn talked fast, and she had a quick smile.

"Oh, sorry," I said.

She led me to our classroom, which she said would be our homeroom. We didn't have homerooms in France.

As we were entering the room, she looked over her shoulder.

"I liked your move back there. You were ready for whatever was about to go down," she said, flashing a sly smile.

"A girl simply must be prepared—that's what I always say," I said. "You were ready, too."

"Girl, I'm always ready," she said. I followed her

into the room, thinking Brooklyn from Harlem was someone I wanted to know more about.

Especially when she looked at the horrid uniform we were wearing and said, "I bet coming from France you're not used to wearing anything as vile as this!"

It was the best I'd felt since arriving in America.

Later that day, we were seated in the dining room eating lunch when a group of girls swooped down on our table. The clear spokeswoman for the girls introduced herself as Marianne Maxwell.

"We just wanted to welcome you to our school," she said. The others nodded, maintaining maximum wattage with their superwhite smiles.

The leader produced a clipboard.

"We are all members of the Leadership Council. We would love to invite you to a meeting," she said.

When I glanced at Brooklyn, she was already shaking her head. Marianne turned to her. The smile appeared to get even brighter.

"Brooklyn, of course you are welcome, too. I'm sure you'd make a fabulous leader. Someday." Marianne's lips seemed to tremble from the force of the smile. I glanced at Brooklyn again, who looked tempted to smack Marianne with the clipboard.

I said, "It's nice to meet you, Marianne, but I will think about your offer. Right now I'm not looking for any new leadership opportunities, as I have so many already. But thank you for asking."

Marianne's eyes did a bug-out sort of thing, then, in a swirl of plaid skirts and overpowering body sprays, the girls were gone.

Brooklyn gave a half smile.

"I was sure they would hypnotize you with their extrawhite teeth and take you back to their planet, wherever that is," she said. I shrugged at Brooklyn and returned to my lunch.

Maybe there was a chance living in New York City had more to offer than simply spying. I might like it here after all. At least until I found Mama.

Then I would do everything I could for us to return home!

CHAPTER 8

Papa had hired a dance student named Rainbow to be my after-school companion. I loved Papa for not calling her my babysitter. He and Cécile would be swamped for the next few weeks preparing for a big dinner for museum staff and volunteers.

That meant Miss Rainbow was in charge of picking me up from school and taking me to ballet class.

Rainbow wasn't much taller than me, but her shaved haircut, ebony skin, and high cheekbones gave her supermodel looks.

Still, she talked and talked and sometimes forgot I wasn't a baby. But I was patient.

I dressed quickly and was a little nervous. Butterflies were expected when starting classes with a new teacher. Even Rainbow said so.

The ballet room was on the second floor overlooking Columbus Avenue. Down below, traffic moved steadily and shops filled with people buying deli sandwiches, sipping coffee, and reading newspapers. Instead of stretching—ballet teachers always wanted you to stretch—I slipped my sketchbook out of my dance bag and quickly tried to capture a few of the faces on the street below. Who knew what kind of danger lurked nearby!

"*Milaya!*" exclaimed a woman who swept into the room, her arms outstretched toward me. I glanced at Rainbow, who looked amused and gave me a shrug.

The woman came toward me and drew me into a hug. She held my face and took a step back.

"Thank you, but my name is Jada, not Mi-la-ya."

She had warm brown eyes and a broad grin. Her words curled with her slight Russian accent.

"No, Jada, of course. *Milaya* is a way to greet

young girls in my country. It's like 'sweetheart.' You don't remember me, no?"

I shook my head.

She introduced herself as Miss Galiana and explained that I used to take lessons from her with Mama. Then her expression saddened. "I was so very sad to hear of the...accident."

"Thank you," I replied.

We spent the next hour doing stretches and movements. I'd missed several weeks of practice before leaving Bordeaux. I couldn't believe how stiff I'd become.

By the time we were done, I was sweaty and tired and ready for a cool beverage. Coke was my favorite, but I was allowed only one a week. I wondered if Rainbow knew that. She had spent the entire lesson on her phone.

I was at the window, filling my dance bag.

"You did very well, my dear," said Miss Galiana. "Your form needs some work, but your concentration is very good, yes?"

"Thank you," I said.

When she stepped away, my attention moved to the street below. A figure stared back at me. I pressed into the window. My breath came in and out in fast gusts.

The man moved to the shadows of one of the buildings.

Then he stepped out, and I caught a brief glimpse. My eyes traced the lines of his profile, the angle of his nose, the tilted oval of his baseball cap. Dark, shadowy with squarish features.

It was him!

The man from the subway!

At the end of the hall were stairs leading to the street. I didn't even hesitate. I raced down them, hit the first floor running.

I burst through the door and into the cool late-afternoon air.

"Hey!" I yelled.

The man froze. He stole a quick glance at me over his shoulder. A flash of skin. African American. Sharply angled face. A UPS truck blared its horn at a taxi. For a second, the large truck blocked my view.

When the truck moved, the man was gone.

I wanted to rush into traffic and follow him. But I didn't get the chance.

"Never do that! Never, ever do that!" Rainbow,

who'd been all zen and Mother Earthy before, was now wide-eyed with worry.

"I'm sorry! I'm sorry!" I said, trying to see past her.

Her brown cheeks had gone ashen. Now the color rushed back and she looked at me. "What happened?" she asked. "Why did you race out of there?"

"I...I saw someone. I mean, I thought I saw someone I know."

She looked up and down the block. Then she took my hand the way a *babysitter* would. Dreadful.

Luckily, we got seats on the train. I took out my sketchbook and immediately sketched as much of the man as I could remember. I would see him again. I was sure of that.

For the next two stops Rainbow rattled on about her artist boyfriend, Dartanyan. She said he was amazing and that he was doing a street art project to go with Papa's big shoe exhibit.

I listened, but not really.

The man outside the dance studio.

He had been in the subway. I was certain.

Was he following me? And if so...why?

CHAPTER 9

Wednesday morning was *très difficile.* At my old school, we did not have classes on Wednesdays. Oh, America. Why must your wool be so itchy and your schools be open on Wednesday?

When did a girl have time to rest and think?

French class with Mademoiselle Louis made my early morning not quite so horrid. In Bordeaux I attended an international school. At first my classes were in English and French. By the time I left, I'd advanced to all-French language education. Because the Proper Day School was not an international school, my French education was simply one class in my overall school day.

I'd been told to "shadow" Brooklyn for the week. Probably because our schedules were almost identical.

"You look tired," she said as we took our seats.

"I am. But I do appreciate you allowing me to follow you around so I don't get lost," I said, placing a notebook on our table. The Proper Day School did not have desks.

Brooklyn arranged her writing journal and pencils on the space in front of her, too. She gave me a crooked smile.

"Girl, you know why they assigned me to you, right?" she said.

I shrugged, ignoring the scratchy itch from the uniform. "For sure it is because our class schedules are so similar, no?"

"They assigned me to show you around because together we represent 39.2 percent of the school's African American population. Yeah, I did the math."

I shrugged again. "I spent the past five years in a little village outside Bordeaux, France. I am quite used to being one of only a few. You must be, too, yes?"

"Yes, but still, I'm just saying. Where I grew up, in Harlem, my neighborhood used to be all black. Then it started changing. And THEN I got a scholarship to come here and my parents were all 'Ooooh, this is amazing' and 'Oh, you should be grateful to be so blessed.'"

Our teacher was starting the lesson.

"*Bonjour, les étudiants*," said Mademoiselle Louis. Brooklyn drew a breath and lowered her voice.

"It was hard starting here in September. Really hard. And hard to leave my friends. I…I'm glad you're here, Jada Sly."

"Me too," I said.

We both smiled, and I felt a warmth right in my heart. I knew what she meant. I was an African American girl who'd lived in a foreign country for a long time. I had all kinds of friends there, but some kids had different ideas. They thought black kids were supposed to act a certain kind of way because that was how we were portrayed in some books and movies.

It was so beyond annoying when kids asked me questions as if I represented all black kids in the whole wide world. Dealing with others' ideas of what

I should be was nothing new. I agreed with Brooklyn: I was glad she was here, too.

Mademoiselle Louis was teaching us funny French phrases. As soon as she told us the theme of the lesson, I began to giggle. I knew that some sayings in French, if you translated them exactly to English words, were pretty funny.

"What makes them so funny?" asked Brooklyn.

She had tried to whisper, but Mademoiselle Louis caught her this time. She stood right in front of us. I expected her to lecture us, but instead, she smiled.

"*Oh la vache!*" said Mademoiselle Louis.

She asked several kids what it meant, but no one came close.

"Jada, you must know this one?" Mademoiselle Louis said.

"It means, literally, 'Oh the cow,'" I said. Everyone laughed. Our teacher smiled.

"That is correct. However, in French, it's the same as when you say 'Oh my goodness.' You say '*Oh la vache*' when you are frustrated," she explained.

In unison, the early-morning French students all shouted, "*Oh la vache!*" We laughed throughout the rest of the lesson.

Hours later, however, what I witnessed was no laughing matter.

It started with the after-school program. The way things worked at the Proper Day School, the last hour to hour and a half was considered a "time for enrichment." Students chose activities that interested them. New students were encouraged to try a variety of things the first week.

"Hey, Jada, would you like to come to my martial arts class today? It's on the first floor," Brooklyn asked.

The instructor, Master Brown, issued me a uniform and a locker. I had trouble opening the locker. Suddenly, a small girl with snow-blond hair appeared.

"Newbies," she said. She gave a big sigh that fluttered her curtain of snowy blond hair. "I'm good with locks—let me." Her pale fingers moved swiftly, and the locker door swung open. But her attitude was as if I'd demanded she help me.

"Uh, okay," I said. "Thank you!" I held the locker door open for just a second. When I looked back where the girl had been, she was gone.

Weird, but nothing compared to what happened next.

I was demonstrating different moves to show Master Brown that I had some training. The small room was wall-to-wall mat. Of course, like all such studios, it smelled like sweaty feet—with just a hint of stale corn chips mixed in.

The tae kwon do studio sat at the front of the building, on the lower level. Central Park sat across the street. Through the window it looked like a postcard.

Master Brown called on a boy who was shorter than me but my same age. His name was Adam. Master Brown wanted Adam to demonstrate the proper way to do an axe kick. I knew the move, but politely listened as he explained.

"It is a kick that does not require the leg to bend. Your power comes from here," Master Brown said, pointing to his midsection, "and here." He indicated to the muscles behind my thighs.

He had us bow to each other. He told me to pay attention.

I did, at least until a flicker of movement in the park caught my eye. Master Brown made a sound, indicating that Adam should begin the kick.

But I was no longer paying attention.

The park...

Across the street.

It was her—again!

Mama. Could it be? I twisted my body for a better look. Seeing her felt like having the wind knocked out of me.

Then I heard a voice.

"Jada!" cried Brooklyn.

I was still squinting at the figure in the park.

When I turned, I felt a breeze move toward my head.

Then a foot slammed into my face.

Dozens of stars twinkled behind my eyes before everything went black.

The last thing I heard as I hit the mat was Brooklyn: "*Oh la vache*, for real!"

Indeed!

CHAPTER 10

Word spread fast about me getting kicked in the face.

I was glad no one bothered asking why I'd been so distracted.

Mama.

It was her. I knew it was.

But why? Why was she sneaking around instead of talking to me?

The next day, soon as I arrived, kids in my home-room gathered around, wanting to see if there was a bruise on my face where I'd been kicked. At least it was a distraction from wondering what was going on with Mama and why she kept popping up in weird places!

A nagging thought tugged at my insides.

What if it isn't real? What if I'm imagining it or something?

I couldn't think like that.

Besides, I had other things to think about. Like the fact that someone had recorded me getting a foot to the face. And sent it to practically THE WHOLE WIDE WORLD.

I thought I would die of embarrassment. A few days in America, and I was a meme. Luckily, my art teacher put an end to it.

Mr. Savant was a tall, elegant man. He moved like a dancer—graceful, purposeful.

"Students, students," he began. He never yelled, but sounded like he was so over the foolishness of students. Still, I liked him. He announced that anyone who showed *any* video of me getting kicked in the head during his class would get automatic detention.

"And write a five-page paper on art appreciation!" he said. "Now pay attention. Today we are learning about Pablo Picasso." Instead of lecturing, he projected a number of works by Picasso onto a screen. Mr. Savant told us to study how Picasso used shapes and color.

"After you've observed these images, I challenge you to use one of these works to inspire a piece of artwork of your own," he said in a funny, dry tone.

He instructed us to go to our class page on the school portal, where we could access the history of whichever painting we chose.

The five works he'd selected were all well known. At least, to me they were. The advantage, I guessed, of being born into a museum family.

The Artist and His Model (1926)

Bathers (1918)

The Old Guitarist (1903)

Le Rêve (1932)

Guernica (1937)

A kid with thick brown hair said, "Mr. Savant, that guy had to be messed up in the head. This stuff looks like something my sister would do. How are we supposed to be inspired by this?"

Mr. Savant got one of those looks my papa gets right before he says he has a headache.

Smiling a smile that did not say happiness, Mr. Savant stood and walked to one of the images.

"Yes, Mr. Burns. It is indeed a misery that Picasso couldn't have been born in the time of *Call of Duty* or reality TV. Instead, he was inspired by many things. In this painting"—he pointed to one filled with points and lines—"he was moved by stories of war. It is called *Guernica*. Look closely, Mr. Burns. It contains a bull, a dead soldier, and a severed hand."

"Really? Cool."

Mr. Savant, who'd been walking away, paused, shook his head, then returned to his desk.

A boy with flaming red hair looked at me, then at the other boy. He smiled and said softly, "Did you know Picasso had twenty-three names?"

I had no answer for that.

"I'm Michael Flannery," he said with a grin. "Most of the twenty-three names came from saints and relatives."

"My name is Sly, Jada Sly," I said quickly, hoping he would not recite all of Picasso's names.

"Nice to meet you, Sly, Jada Sly," he said, still grinning, like he and I were in on some kind of secret.

I smiled back, then melted away into a distant corner of the room, finding a spot on the oversized rug, then sliding down the wall. I took my art journal from my bag.

After being kicked in the face—not to mention being 100 percent sure I'd seen my mother in Central Park—I was happy to have some time to myself to reflect on Picasso's work.

I dragged my fingers across the cottony nap of the drawing paper. It was thick and soft. Quick sketch strokes sprang from my pencil while my brain thought about art, inspiration, and anything else so that I didn't have to think about bad guys lurking in the shadows and vanishing mothers.

I also thought about the African American artist Jackie Ormes. She was definitely someone I admired. Not so much for her art style, but her fearlessness. Her cartoons were popular from the 1930s to the 1950s, appearing in black newspapers. Papa once brought home a book about her for me, and I'd been hooked ever since.

Jackie liked including paper dolls with her comics. The dolls portrayed black women as sophisticated and fashion forward—very different from how we were drawn at the time. Jackie had style and purpose. I liked that.

I chose Picasso's *Le Rêve* painting as my inspiration. I liked all the soft curves and connected lines.

I sketched awhile, then had an idea. What if I combined Picasso's and Ormes's art styles? I could take *Le Rêve*, create a character, and design a few paper doll outfits.

Or what if I put that beautiful figure into a school uniform?

Genius!

I felt pretty good. It was turning out great.

However, creativity did not always solve my problems. I thought I was going to be stuck in a mystery forever.

Was Papa safe? Was I?

I pushed thoughts of Picasso aside and turned to a new page in my art journal. I went through the situation as I'd sketched it out:

> 1. Get to the Braniff Bank Building,
>   where Mr. Tillerson and Mama once
>   worked. The Braniff Bank Building
>   is in Lower Manhattan, nearly
>   the bottom of the NYC map. It is
>   practically a WORLD away.

2. Find Charles "Charlie" Tillerson.
3. And if all that isn't enough, figure out why Mama keeps popping up and then disappearing.
4. Why is the man from the subway station following me? What does he want?
5. Something about the airport attacker keeps nagging at my brain. I have to figure out what it is.

I was getting tired.

For heaven's sake, my jeté was losing its grandness; my ballon had lost its bounce.

Whatever was happening, I was more determined than ever to stop it.

Enough was enough!

Jada Sly, artist and spy, was ready to take her mission to the next level.

CHAPTER 11

On Fridays students set aside school uniforms to wear personal attire.

Free at last!

Naturally I chose my full skirt of red tulle, simple red ballet flats, and a black T-shirt with white lettering that read BLACK GIRL MAGIC to celebrate the occasion. I'm proud of my African American and Egyptian heritage. I was a strong little black woman, Papa liked to say.

Of course, I topped the look off with my smart red scarf and even a beret!

I'd gotten to know Brooklyn pretty well during

the week. So I should not have been the least bit surprised when she arrived wearing a BLACK GIRL MAGIC tee, too.

"What's up, Parlez-Vous?" she said when she saw me.

At the end of the school day, Brooklyn invited me to her last activity again. I groaned.

"I'm not going to get kicked in the face again, am I?"

She shrugged. "Not unless you want to!"

Wasn't the answer I was looking for, but I followed her anyway.

Brooklyn led me quietly past clusters of students headed here and there. She clasped my wrist and tugged me along.

"What kind of club is it?" I asked, but she placed one finger over her lips.

"Shhh! Top secret!" she said. I giggled.

She did not.

Moving swiftly past students milling near open doorways, we made a sharp left toward an end room. The door was closed. Brooklyn turned the knob. She stepped aside, facing me with a triumphant look glittering behind her red-framed glasses.

When I saw what was on the whiteboard at the front of the room, I stood there, confused.

Written in crisp penmanship with green dry-erase marker: INTERNATIONAL PIE SOCIETY.

Okay, for some reason, Brooklyn thought I was into pies. How could I tell her I was more of a crème brûlée kind of girl?

"Oh," I said, "pie?"

She had been facing me. She turned to the board and gestured to a boy standing beside it.

"Big Mike, c'mon, man!" she said. "The sign?"

I realized it was the kid from art class. Brooklyn looked back at me, tugged me deeper into the room, and made sure the door locked behind us.

"Sorry," said Big Mike. He wore an apron and held a large mixing spoon. On the red-and-white-checked apron was a printed circle that looked like a badge. It read INTERNATIONAL PIE SOCIETY.

"Kill the lights," he said solemnly.

All the electronic humming seemed louder in the semidarkness. Brooklyn gave me a yank, turning me to face the board.

On the screen was a picture of a pie with a sign

taped over it. Written in the same evenly spaced glowing lettering over the word "PIE":

SPY (SOCIETY OF PROVOCATEUR YOUTHS).

"Invisible ink," Big Mike said, pointing to the glowing letters. "We make our own. And we use this to light it up." He held up a black light.

Brooklyn flipped the light switch on, eliminating the carefully camouflaged words.

I noticed several things:

First, the room held a small kitchen that included an oven, sink, and cabinets.

Next, there were two other students present. A girl and a boy.

And there was an old woman wearing white gloves, who sat napping in a comfortable chair covered in a cozy toile print. (The chair, not the woman.)

"C. J. Ellis Effingham the Fourth," said a tall boy from our homeroom. "I read in the *Times* that your family is spending over ten million on renovations to the Sly. My father's business just had a thirty-million-dollar expansion."

Say what? Even I didn't know how much the renovations were costing. Who was this kid? He smiled wide and shook my hand as if we were old friends.

Michael came over. He said, "CJ has the gift of gab. He's a people person kind of guy. Everybody calls *me* Big Mike. Um, you might not know this, but the Smithsonian Museum in Washington, DC, is spending two billion on renovations—"

"MICHAEL!" Brooklyn yelled. She sounded exasperated and looked it, too, pushing her red-framed glasses up the bridge of her nose with force.

"Sorry, sorry, sorry," Big Mike said, before continuing with the introductions. "The woman sleeping over there is Mrs. Moldy, our staff chaperone. We try not to disturb her."

He pointed to a girl with snow-blond hair combed over her face. "That's Hadley over there." It was the girl from the locker room, the one who picked the lock and disappeared before I could thank her.

Hadley gave me a head bob, then looked me up and down like she wasn't sure she could trust me. Then she turned her head, letting that curtain of snow-blond hair cover her face.

"Had's family is on that reality show. The one

with the famous blond sisters and their crazy mom," Big Mike said.

I looked back at her. I said, "I've watched it a few times. Never saw you on it."

She slid back the curtain of hair to show both startlingly blue eyes, and said, "And you never will."

Brooklyn said, "Hadley's quiet, but not shy. Just not exactly quick to trust people."

Taking it all in, I asked, "Is all of this for real?"

"The realest," said Brooklyn. "Welcome to the Proper Day School's secret society of spies."

The next hour went by fast!

I asked how they figured out that I was a spy, too. CJ said they'd watched me watch our fellow classmates.

Big Mike said he sneaked a few looks over my shoulder in art class.

"You seem to have a knack for faces," he said. "A great skill for spies."

Hadley did her hair-flicking thing. She was sitting on one chair with her feet on another. She said,

"You seemed decent enough. You weren't all desperate for friends or getting in other people's business. We figured you weren't a puppet like some of these other dweebs are."

Neither a "puppet" nor a "dweeb." Well, yay me!

"I told them how you shot down Marianne Maxwell and her leadership drones in the dining hall," Brooklyn said. "We were all impressed by that."

She also said that, despite being kicked in the face, I'd handled myself pretty well in martial arts class.

Then they all shared a look.

"We get the feeling something is wrong," Brooklyn said. I was touched by their concern. And a bit surprised that anyone had been paying attention to me or was able to tell something was wrong.

I chewed my lip. How embarrassing! A good spy needed to be covert—not show everyone how she was feeling.

Brooklyn seemed to read my thoughts.

"We're trained observers, so don't feel bad," she said.

"Trained by who?" I asked.

"By whom." Big Mike corrected me.

"Big Mike, I'm warning you!" said Brooklyn.

"Oh, sorry," he said, and grinned. His smirk did not look sorry.

"We trained ourselves," Hadley said in a low voice. "Each of us got used to practicing spy skills alone. Now we get together and practice with each other."

They got the idea for the International PIE Society, a.k.a. SPY, at the beginning of the school year. Students were encouraged to join groups or form their own. Inspired by Big Mike's love of desserts, they decided to form their own cooking club.

Instead of joining the Food and Nutrition Club, Big Mike and Hadley convinced the fifth-grade dean to allow a club dedicated to pies.

"I told her pie had social and historical value in American society," Big Mike said.

"So, how do you pull it off? You know, convincing the dean and everybody that this really is a group interested in making pies?" I said.

"Because it really is!" Brooklyn said. "We meet twice a week. Thanks to Big Mike's talent for baking and Hadley's family connections—you know, her family owns the X Hotels—we have bakers and their assistants volunteering to come in once a month and teach us baking techniques."

I'd stayed in those hotels all over the world. I knew from the reality show that the famous family owned them.

"They've all known each other since pre-K. My first day here, Big Mike was my student guide," Brooklyn said.

"Yeah," Big Mike said. "Five minutes after I met her, she hacked my phone."

"I said I was sorry. When I'm feeling anxious or worried, I code," Brooklyn said.

CJ jumped in. "We've made our own rules," he said. "Father says any organization that wants to be successful has to set rules and goals for itself. He's a very smart businessman."

"He makes Zoodle Doodle cheese puffs," Brooklyn said with a head shake and a sigh.

"He's a financial genius!" CJ retorted.

Big Mike said, "My dad is a detective for the NYPD. I'm here on scholarship. I like investigating—analyzing information to figure out what it means."

Hadley said she was the lock picker of the group, while CJ's talent was the ability to talk his way out of or into just about anything.

"Thanks to Mom and Dad, I have access to some

of the biggest names in New York City," he said. "And I've learned that the right story told with confidence is guaranteed to get you into anyplace you want to go."

Brooklyn laughed. "He's going to make a great politician—"

"Or excellent con man," I said. I blushed, realizing I'd said my thought aloud. I didn't know him well and didn't want to sound mean. But he looked at me and beamed, then took a bow.

Big Mike produced a list of the rules. It read:

1. The No. 1 rule of spying—intelligence first! Gathering information to decide what is our top priority. Without intel or information, we have nothing!
2. Identify the suspicious person/thing.
3. Observe the subject.
4. Remain vigilant. Good operatives must maintain their cover.
5. Meet back at headquarters. It is time to evaluate all the information gathered to determine what it means and/or where it leads.

6. If you're unable to uncover information about the subject, consider they may not be as they appear. If they are in disguise or using an alias, return to rule No. 1.
7. If information shows the subject is not a threat, the case is closed. If the subject requires more observation, it may be time to expose the subject to higher authorities.
8. If the police or other agencies fail to act, a good operative Must Take Action!

"Wow!" I said after reading the rules. "You guys are awesome. These rules are great! I think I'm going to like being a member of the International PIE Society."

"The best part," Hadley said, eyes obscured by her hair, "is no one suspects the spy part exists!"

I looked over at Mrs. Moldy.

"What about her?" I said.

CJ smirked. "Each club is supposed to have an adult chaperone. She's ours. Perfect, if you ask me."

Brooklyn made a palms-up gesture. "The less the

adults know, the better," she said. "We need to keep everything as secret as possible. One day, we might have a real mission."

I nodded.

That day could be here sooner than any of them thought!

CHAPTER 12

International Pie Society

Saturday.

After I got over the initial shock of finding out my new school had a secret organization, I asked the members of SPY to meet me at the Sly.

I felt a jumble of things inside—scared, excited, nervous, relieved. I decided to dress in ultra-spy mode: a long-sleeved black tee that fell past my bottom, covering the waist of my black leggings.

Having Brooklyn include me in their secret society felt amazing.

However, I had a problem:

How could I get them to help me if I wasn't ready to tell them about my mission to find Mama?

After tossing and turning all night, I made a decision. I knew how I wanted to handle things with the International PIE Society.

I was moving toward the front door to wait for my friends when something Papa said made me stop.

He was adding a collection of several Degas paintings to the shoe exhibit, including *Three Dancers in Red Costume*.

I felt a slight shiver.

The beautiful Degas paintings were heading to our exhibit hall. It was like kismet. Like a sign about Mama. I thought about the postcard in the Chanel bag.

Now more than ever, I had things to discuss with my fellow spies.

I led them to a tiny storage space right behind the children's parlor. A village of boxes, dust-covered toys, and forgotten treasures surrounded us. It was like being inside our very own HQ.

CJ looked appraisingly around the room. He sighed. "I'll bet real spies meet in places far worse than this!"

"Hey!" said Brooklyn. "Don't be rude. This is… nice."

CJ fluffed his hair and said, "I wasn't knocking this place. It's just that my dad says real-life spies don't make a lot of money, unless they steal it from a hostile nation."

"CJ, must you always look for business opportunities?" Brooklyn said, rolling her eyes.

"Making money is not a crime. My father likes to say—"

"Effingham, can we leave your daddy out of things right now? It's too early for Zoodle Doodles," Hadley drawled.

Since learning of the group's existence, I'd been wondering if they could—or would—help me with my problem.

How would I manage my spy mission alone? Maybe I didn't have to.

Making a big sigh, I said, "I have a problem. Do you think you guys might be able to help me with a real spy mission?"

That got everyone's complete and undivided attention.

Brooklyn pulled her knees up, wrapping her arms around them. She sat staring intently at me.

I opened my red leather sketchbook. A tiny dust speck floated past, and Hadley let out a huge sneeze.

"You know—" began Big Mike. The others all groaned, but he kept on. "It was once rumored that the heart stops every time you sneeze, thus causing people to say 'God bless you.' Only, that's not quite true. In fact—"

"Spare us the PBS special, would ya?" said Brooklyn. "Jada, what's your mission?"

I went through the sketchbook, describing the mystery so far. However, I did leave out one thing— the fact that I thought Mama was alive.

Here was what I knew:

- Mama's plane crashed in April.
- Before she left for her trip, she received a mysterious phone call.
- The call was from a man named Charles Tillerson, I believed.

•   *She wrote his name and the number*
     21 on the back of a Degas postcard.

I told them more about Charles Tillerson and sketched an image of how I remembered him.

"Cool drawing," Hadley said. She trailed her fingers over the black inked lines.

"Thanks. When I sketch, it helps me think," I said.

"But, Parlez-Vous—uh, Jada, how do you know this Mr. Tillerson dude has anything to do with your mom's plane crash?" Brooklyn said.

Big Mike added, "Yeah. What if that Charles guy wasn't on the phone that day? What if it was someone else giving her *his* name?"

I'd thought of that, too.

"Then," I said, "it still means that a call about Charles was the last message she received at our house. And it's all I've got. Papa is so determined to 'protect me' from everything. I can't get any real information."

"Pa-*pa*," Brooklyn said with a giggle.

"What?"

She grinned. "Sorry. You don't call him Daddy

93

like the rest of us would. You pronounce it 'pa-pahhh.' Girl, being with you makes me feel like I'm in a movie!"

Everyone laughed, including me.

"Where did your mother work with him?" Hadley's soft voice floated.

I turned to her, pushing the sketchbook toward her. I had written down the name.

"The Caspian Group, Inc.," I said.

"It's a small publishing company," Hadley said. She'd googled it on her phone already. "But I don't see any other information about it."

"That's weird, right?" I said. "All I know is that when Mama worked there, she worked with Mr. Tillerson, on the twenty-first floor of the Braniff Bank Building."

"Your mother was a banker?" said CJ, his ears perking up.

"Pay attention, CJ!" said Brooklyn. "They have all sorts of offices in those big bank buildings. She worked for a publishing place that had offices on the twenty-first floor. Right?"

"Right!" I said.

"So you want to . . . *what*?" CJ asked. Even when

he was being helpful, he had a knack for sounding snooty.

"I want to go down to that office building and talk to Charles Tillerson. I want to see if he knows why a call from him or about him made Mama antsy the last time I saw her. I want to know if he knows…" My voice caught in my throat.

"Parlez-Vous, it's okay. I know how terrible it must be to lose your mom. But your mom left that job five years ago. What if he doesn't work there anymore?" Brooklyn asked.

I shrugged. "Then I'll have to look for someone else."

"We need to figure out how to get more intel. That's what we need to do instead," Big Mike said.

CJ smirked. He said, "Well, if all you want is to visit the Braniff Bank Building, no problem."

"Big problem," I said. "It's at the bottom of the island." Then he ticked an eyebrow at me. One that said *Ah, yes*.

We began to hatch a plan.

If it worked, I would be one step closer to getting answers!

I led them on a tour of the museum even though

it wasn't open to the public. Perks of being the director's daughter and all that. I told them about the guy in the hoodie who tried to mug me at the airport and about the man in the baseball cap who I thought was following me.

But I did not tell them about Mama popping up.

"Intrigue does seem to follow you," said Big Mike.

The Black Victorians' Room on the second floor was always one of my favorites. Old-fashioned gilt-framed photos of all sizes hung on the walls and covered shelf tops. Each held a photo of African Americans and Black Brits wearing their finery from the nineteenth and early twentieth centuries.

I pointed to a photo of a stern-looking man with medium-dark skin and a huge mustache.

"That's my great-great-grandfather Benjamin Sly," I said. "It's because of him the museum exists." I shared stories I'd grown up hearing. How Benjamin Sly, son of former slaves, managed to work three jobs. He and his brother, William, bought property and managed to stay afloat during the hardships of the Great Depression.

"It's very impressive what your ancestors were able to do, given the politics at that time," said a voice.

We all spun to find an older man in an old-fashioned hat. He wore a buttery yellow sweater and pocket watch on a chain. He also carried a walking stick. When he saw our matching quizzical stares, he released a burst of laughter that made us immediately feel at ease.

"Please, forgive my intrusion. Albert Cheswick, at your service," he said in the most delightful British accent. "I am one of the volunteers here and happened to overhear your chat."

He turned to me and continued. "I take it you are the daughter of our fearless leader, Dr. Benjamin Sly the Third?"

"Yes, I am. It is very good to meet you," I said. The rest of the group waved hello.

Mr. Cheswick said, "Are you fine young people here as part of some school project? Getting a behind-the-scenes look, as it were?" He barked another round of laughter that sounded so funny it made us laugh, too.

Big Mike glanced in my direction, then turned to Mr. Cheswick. "Jada is new at our school, and we're getting to know her and this cool place. I thought I'd been to every museum in New York City, but I'd never been here before today."

Brooklyn said, "Well, I have. My mom and pops are all about Black History and knowing about the great accomplishments of our people. Never in a million years did I think I'd be going to school with you, though, Jada Sly!"

Mr. Cheswick said good-bye and disappeared around the corner.

I remembered that Papa wanted to meet my friends. I led them up to his office.

When we reached the third floor, I noticed that Papa's door wasn't quite shut. I held my finger to my lips, signaling them to be quiet.

Instantly, we all dropped into a crouch. They looked at me suspiciously.

I whispered, "I think someone is in Papa's office, but the lights aren't on."

"How do you know it's not him?" Hadley's quiet voice asked.

"Papa has bad eyesight. Even with his contacts, he needs a lot of light to see."

So we all crept along the hallway until we were outside his door.

"Papa!" I called out, pushing the door open and walking quickly inside. Not at all expecting to find him rummaging around his own office. In the dark.

Brooklyn reached behind me and raked her hand along the wall for a light switch. She found one and clicked it. Pale overhead light filtered down. Glowing like a guilty moon was one pale face. All black clothing. Hair as pale as frost. It was the guy from two Fridays ago. The one who'd arrived at the museum when the alarm went off.

He stood straight and tall, his blue eyes assessing each of our faces before turning to me.

"Jada," he said. His tone was polite but chilly. "We meet again!"

"What exactly are you looking for, Mr. Highborne?" I said.

Before he could answer, Papa's voice rose up behind me.

"Jada! And you brought your friends. Highborne! You're here! My daughter is visiting today, and these are her new friends," Papa said. "Hello, children."

They all said hello.

I turned to find Mr. Highborne studying me. At first I didn't understand. Then I realized he was clenching something in his hand that he didn't want me to see.

What was he hiding?

CHAPTER 13

I wondered where Mama was. Was she safe? Did she miss me?

Papa and I were entering the subway station. It was Monday morning. As we boarded the train, he was talking about ancient shoes, but my mind was filled with other things.

Like what had Allister Highborne been looking for in Papa's office?

And would Charles Tillerson even remember me or Mama?

The train pulled into our stop. Papa tucked the

New York Times under his arm and reached for my hand. Bodies pushed against us. We were in a wave of people flowing from the subway to the outside world.

One thing I'd learned since arriving in NYC was that riding the subway first thing in the morning was serious business. People walked fast. Everyone was in a hurry. Keeping your feet moving was very important. Every morning it made my heart race, trying to keep pace. Papa placed a hand on my shoulder to guide me.

Glancing around, noticing angular chins, rounded cheeks, triangular haircuts, and boxy heads, I was enjoying the geometry of life and how it made all our faces different. At least, I enjoyed it until a familiar shape came into view.

Carefully, I paused, looking over my shoulder. Thin as a silhouette, but squarish, the figure ducked behind one of the huge cement columns.

I tried looking again, but the morning commuters stumbling to get past me pushed me away from Papa's grasp. I felt myself getting jostled around.

Then I turned and looked right at a faceless shade hidden in the folds of a hoodie.

No mistaking it this time. Not the squarish man

I'd seen here before—the man I'd spotted at the ballet studio wearing the baseball cap.

No. Not him.

But I had seen *this* man before. The odd feeling that something wasn't quite right flashed in my head.

He was the thief from outside the airport.

"Jada!" My father's voice drifted down from the steps leading out of the underground tunnel.

When I turned in Papa's direction, Hoodie shoved into me.

I stumbled backward. Someone else caught me and stepped around me.

"Papa!" I yelled.

He was racing down the steps, and I turned to run up and away from the stranger.

Papa clasped my shoulders, looking me over.

"What happened? Are you all right?" he asked. His gaze swept anxiously over my face, searching for signs of distress. I had to be practically dripping distress.

"Papa! It was him!" I said. "Did you see that?" My heart grew tighter. If I wasn't careful, I'd go into a full panic attack. I didn't want that to happen.

"See what, *petite lapine*?" His tone was concerned.

"The thief from the airport was following us."

"Are you sure?" he asked. "You'll give yourself a panic attack."

Him mentioning my attacks made me angry. Then, that was when I realized something else. My backpack was open. I shook it, my hands flailing around.

"It's gone!" I said, fighting back tears.

"What is?" he said.

"My sketchbook. It's gone. That man took it. He had to have."

We looked around for it, but quickly realized it was nowhere to be seen.

"Oh, baby, you probably left it on the train," Papa said.

"No! I didn't. The man took it. It was the same man from the airport. He's following me," I blurted out. I was almost panting with frustration.

Papa made a face. He looked like I was trying to feed him raw liver. (Papa did not even like cooked liver.)

"Jada!" His voice was low. He moved me away from the stairs and looked at me with hard eyes that made me feel cold inside. "I've told you, no more of this spy business," he said.

"But I'm not playing a game! Papa, haven't you

ever, even for one moment, thought that there was something not right about Mama's so-called plane crash? Like maybe we weren't told the truth?"

"Your mother," he said. His voice sounded strained. His eyes had bugged out of his head. "What truth? What does your sketchbook have to do with your mother? Or this phantom man from the airport!"

The anger that had flickered in his gaze vanished. He covered his face. When he removed his hands, his eyes were damp and sad.

"Jada," he said, "your mother boarded a private plane that she was flying, and crashed shortly after taking off from New York City. I know it's horrible. I know it's hard to accept. But your mom died."

"But Papa..."

"But what?"

"I...I saw her? I've seen her."

"Saw who?" he whispered.

I swallowed hard. My words came out in a whisper at first, too. Then louder and louder until I was nearly shouting.

"Mama. I saw her. At the airport. I saw Mama!"

"Just like you saw the man who tried to mug you?

The same man who followed you to the subway to steal your sketchbook."

I rubbed my elbow. My arm felt sore where the man had shoved me before pushing out of the way.

"Papa..." My tone was pleading.

He pulled me into a hug and held me tight.

"Jada..."

Tears filled my eyes, but I quickly wiped them away.

He tried again, "Jada..."

"Forget I said anything!" I yelled. Then I turned and ran up the stairs, away from the hissing and screeching of the trains.

Mr. Savant decided we were going outside to sketch. I was grateful. The incident in the subway had left me angry and frustrated. It felt good to be in the cool autumn air.

Golden leaves danced above our heads.

"Please, students, do me a favor. Resist the urge to liberate yourselves. If you wander off, I shall report you to Mrs. Gnarly, the headmistress," he said.

Our assignment for the day was to sketch the

trees. Luckily, Mama sent me more than one sketch-book since that hoodie creep took my other one.

Our class was only eight people. We spread out and found an angle on what we wanted to draw by the Jacqueline Kennedy Onassis Reservoir. Jacqueline Kennedy was a woman of immense style and was once married to President John F. Kennedy. We spread a blanket on the ground. I wondered what it would be like to live such a fabulous life that you get a divine reservoir in gorgeous Central Park named after you.

Mr. Savant's voice cut into my wondering. He told us to quickly sketch block shapes into place before going back and slowly turning each shape into an actual object.

"Can I sit with you, Parlez-Vous?" Brooklyn said. I nodded.

"You seem down," she went on.

Brooklyn's expression was so genuine and warm I almost broke down and told her everything.

Instead, I shrugged, saying, "I'm fine. A little aggravated. Parents can be exhausting."

She let out a laugh. "Now, that's the truth!"

After a little while, I was engrossed in turning my blocks and shapes into trees and fountains. Brooklyn and I were playfully making comments about Mr. Savant.

"He's so funny," she said.

"He's a little cranky," I said. "But he is funny, too."

We both giggled. Mr. Savant had gone over to a couple of students who were supposed to be drawing trees but were instead making duck noises. Joggers raced past, their colorful outfits brighter than the changing leaf colors. Brooklyn gave me a look over the red plastic rims of her glasses.

Just at that moment, my attention was drawn to the opposite direction.

Beneath a thicket of old trees with fat yellow leaves, someone was hiding. My body went tense, and my hands gripped the pencil so tightly I thought it might break. A partially shielded face disappeared into the shadows. She—I could not say for sure it was a she, only I had this feeling—stared forward—in my direction.

Sunlight glinted off the reservoir. I squinted hard. The woman pressed closer into the tree. Stripes of shade fell across her face and body. I blinked, feeling like the sun had to be playing tricks on me....

It wasn't. My breath caught in my throat.

I saw her.

Mama.

She was really there this time.

Without another word, I dashed into the woods.

I didn't bother looking back. I knew I'd get into big trouble for leaving class, but after what had happened in the subway, I needed proof.

For some reason, Mama thought it was necessary to keep watch over me from the shadows. But doing so was making me crazy; I couldn't take it anymore.

So I ran.

And so did she.

Somewhere behind me, voices were rising up. The woman ahead of me, who I thought was Mama, was moving faster. I made my body dig into all the energy it had. My stomach muscles cramped as I pushed harder to find the strength to keep running.

Now we were no longer darting back and forth from behind trees and bushes—we were sprinting toward Summit Rock. I was moving as fast as I could toward the stone benches in that part of the park.

Even as I raced along, however, I knew from a lifetime of experience that when Mama wanted to run, she could run!

The path twisted sharply, and when I turned, I was face-to-face with about a dozen students. Another Proper Day School class.

A blur of khaki, a Burberry trench coat, darted into view. A smear of yellow taxi appeared as well.

Mama paused to glance over the top of the cab.

Just for a second.

And then she was gone—again.

CHAPTER 14

Apparently, when you leave class without permission, it is equal to making babies cry or tearing that little tag off a mattress, the one that says REMOVAL OF THIS TAG COULD LEAD TO FEDERAL PROSECUTION.

The dean of fifth-grade students, Mrs. Vicario, had been waiting for me when I came into the building without the rest of my class. They'd already returned and reported my escape.

I didn't care how much trouble I got into.

Mama was alive. She was in hiding and still keeping an eye on me. But she was ALIVE!

Mrs. Vicario held open the side door, told me she was glad to see I was all right, then asked me to come to her office after school.

A good spy must always keep her composure.

Mr. Savant had come up to me and said, "Young lady, if you want to give me a heart attack, please have the decency to do it with greasy foods. Running away during class is just plain rude!"

Later, at her office, Mrs. Vicario must have decided that our dilemma could best be handled over tea and baked goods, which was how I wound up in front of her desk sipping a delightful vanilla-mint blend while eating a flaky chocolate croissant. My favorites.

Mrs. Vicario was a small woman with a bun of dark brown hair. Her hands moved in shaky motions like a wind-up toy with stops and starts. Rings glittered on one hand, and bracelets jangled from the opposite wrist. Her smiles flashed on and off like neon lights at an amusement park. I could tell they were meant to be reassuring. However, her lips sliding out and in, in and out, made her smiles jump in quick and jittery movements, same as her hands.

"Jada, I am so sorry I wasn't here to greet you last

week when you arrived," she said. Her lips quivered like bunny whiskers. I thought of Josephine Baker—the bunny, not the singer.

I said to her, "You are a busy woman. But thank you," because I did not know what else to say.

We exchanged smiles and continued making small talk that felt like a code. Blink once if you feel awkward; twice if you wish you were someplace else. We sat like that for a few moments, just blinking and sipping tea.

Then she hit me with the two most terrifying words ever:

Your grandmother.

Now Mrs. Vicario's winks, blinks, flutters, and smiles found a rhythm, like an SOS. "Lady Sly is on the board of our school," Mrs. Vicario said.

"She is not a titled lady," I said, although it was easy to picture my grandmother making people bow at her pointy-toed shoes and call her Lady Sly.

Mrs. Vicario's voice cut into my thoughts. "Your grandmother has raised so much money for our school and done so many outstanding things for the arts community, I'd call her Queen Mother if she wanted!"

The administrator appeared surprised at her own words and slapped a ringed-fingered hand over her lips. She released an almost hysterical laugh, then drew herself up high in her seat.

Once she regained control of herself, she said, "I'm sure you didn't mean to cause a disruption this morning, Jada. We are tasked with keeping all of you safe, therefore we can't have any students rushing away from their classes unsupervised."

"I understand," I said, setting down the saucer with the remains of the croissant. I took another sip of tea. My fingers did their best not to shake. How much trouble was I going to be in?

Her eyes widened when she seemingly read my thoughts. "Oh no, dear. You are not in trouble. You're new. New," she said. It felt like she was trying to convince someone else. A silence fell over the room. Ticking from a small grandfather clock sounded thick in the space. We both sipped from our teacups.

She went on:

"Good. Now, if you need any unscheduled breaks in the future, please don't hesitate to come down and find me. I'd be happy to assist."

Then, leaning forward, she added, "Don't worry, your grandmother asked me to look after you. I understand you've had a most difficult time." With that, her voice grew soft and her smile wary.

Obviously, Grandmother Sly had told her I was fragile and needed special care.

I managed to pull yet another wobbly smile into place. Since it worked so well before, all I said was "Thank you."

We nodded. "You may go home, Jada. Remember, if you need anything, ask me."

All I could think about was how my barely five-foot-tall, one-hundred-pound grandmother easily bullied an upstanding school authority figure in such a manner.

I headed out the school doors and told myself, *Don't look, don't look, don't look* as I passed the glass doors to the courtyard beyond. If Mama's shadowy figure had returned, I didn't want to know.

CHAPTER 15

I arrived at school the next day feeling determined.

"What's poppin', Parlez-Vous? Is everything all right?" said Brooklyn.

I'd been awake most of the night, my brain going over what had happened yesterday at school. *Was it Mama?*

"Can I tell you something?" I asked. All of a sudden, the secret I'd kept hidden scratched at my insides. I needed to talk to someone.

"I told this to Papa, and he flipped," I said.

"So tell me," she said, calmly. We found a quiet

spot by the wrought-iron benches, away from the noise of students being dropped off. I told her—about seeing Mama in the park, about my belief that Mama was a real-life spy, and how this all tied into the postcard clue.

Brooklyn listened intently. Her reaction was totally unexpected. When I finished, she hugged me and said, "I believe you. So what are we going to do about it?"

As I hugged her back, I realized how much stronger I felt to not be totally alone.

"She's here, Brooklyn," I said as she continued to hold me. "I know it. I *saw* her. Papa wouldn't believe me if I told him. Please, no one else can know. Okay?"

"One hundred percent, it's just you and me!" she said.

I blew out a breath. I told her how upset Papa had gotten about my spying, and my thoughts and feelings on the crash.

"Parents try so hard, but sometimes they just don't get it," Brooklyn said flatly. "Secret agent life can get lonely. That's why we formed the International PIE Society."

Ha ha. Pie. We both looked at each other and laughed.

"Still, I'm not certain what to do," I admitted.

"That doesn't sound like you, Parlez-Vous!"

I smiled, saying, "So, that's a thing now? Parlez-Vous?"

"Fo' sho'." She laughed. Then she sat up straight and said, "Listen, I know you're new here and life has been different, but the best thing for us to do is to keep working on the mission—figuring out how to get in touch with this Charles dude. One step at a time, Parlez-Vous. One step at a time!"

By the end of the school day, we were ready to put our plan in action.

Big Mike's brain might have a lot of random facts, but when it came time to make a strategy, he took charge.

He went over the plan:

We were taking a tour of CJ's father's headquarters. It stood directly across the street from the Braniff Bank Building.

Rainbow was meeting up with Hadley's baby-sitter, Estelle. They were going to take us downtown on the subway. CJ's nanny would be waiting at the corporate office.

Big Mike leaned over the kitchen countertop like a general. Holding his favorite spatula, he stabbed it in our direction.

"Now, we need to talk it out. Everyone needs to know how this is going to work," he said. "CJ. Go!"

"The tour takes roughly thirty minutes, but it's the movie at the end that is the key," CJ said.

The plan was for me to sneak out during the movie. I already had a bag packed with what I'd need to help me at the Braniff Bank Building.

"Questions? Comments? Concerns?" Big Mike asked, his normally soft face hard with seriousness. He said our sitters and companions would take us downtown by subway. He said we could strategize along the way.

CJ looked scared.

"Dude, come on," Brooklyn said. "Don't tell me you've never been on a subway before." Her lopsided grin was for sure a dare.

"Of course I have. I mean, well, Laura," he said in his poshest tone, "doesn't happen to like the subway. She's my nanny. We usually take one of the cars."

We all laughed at how delightfully red his cheeks turned as he sputtered out his explanation. CJ, with all his stuffy airs, had fears just like the rest of us.

Rainbow and Estelle met us in front of the Proper Day School. They insisted on treating us like kindergarteners on a class trip.

Rainbow led the way while Estelle walked behind us. We took an express train and were lucky to find seats. By the time we reached midtown, the train was packed and we could barely move. It took us forty-five minutes to get downtown.

We exited the train at Bowling Green Station and headed toward the big building with the gigantic Zoodle Doodle on top.

Everything went according to plan. We took the tour. We laughed politely at all the guide's jokes. When it was time to watch the movie, I didn't think I could bear the smell of another salty snack.

"You convinced Rainbow she could wait in the conference room with the other nannies, right?" Brooklyn whispered.

"Yes," I answered, my voice tight. The tension was building.

This was it.

My entire mission rested on how I handled the next ten or fifteen minutes.

"Don't forget this," Brooklyn said, sliding a duffel my way and tearing me from my thoughts.

It was Hadley's idea that I'd need a change of clothes.

"You can't go in there looking like some kid. I brought you something sophisticated," she said.

Big Mike said, "Look inside. The folder was my idea."

"Mine too!" argued Brooklyn.

Big Mike rolled his eyes, then stabbed his spatula in the general direction of the folder. He'd been waving that thing around since we left Proper Country Day. He was so proud to have collected all the information he thought I'd need to navigate the Braniff Bank Building.

"In buildings like those, you have to be on a list, or they won't let you past the elevators," he said.

Brooklyn took over again. "And because I'm the tech master for this bunch, I was able to hack my way in and leave your name as a guest for Mr. Chambers on the twenty-first floor. And when they call him to verify..." Her voice was high-pitched and singsongy. Uh-oh. What had she done?

Hadley said, "Security will call this number, and we'll give the okay."

"But—" I began.

Hadley pointed at Brooklyn. "Master, remember. She messed with their phones."

"Who is Mr. Chambers?" asked CJ.

They all turned and glared at him. Hadley, in her soft voice, said, "He doesn't exist. We made him up."

It took only a few minutes to escape from the Zoodle Doodle headquarters. Soon I was standing on a grassy patch of lawn wedged between two enormous office buildings. I'd already changed from what I was wearing to what had been inside the very chic duffel—no doubt from Hadley's closet, as well.

Across Beaver Street stood a shimmering highrise. The ground-floor sign was black granite.

BRANIFF BANK BUILDING.

Next stop, the twenty-first floor!

CHAPTER 16

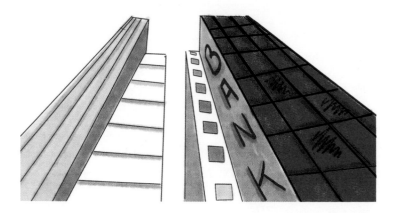

"Good afternoon, I am here to see Mr. Chambers," I said. I tried to look as grown-up and calm as possible. Truly, my insides were shaking. But I told myself, *Remember the mission.*

The guard in black and blue was impossibly tall. He looked me over, taking in my—Hadley's—cashmere suit, a pale linen color. I wore matching tights and flats. No doubt her mom had bought the outfit for mother-daughter teas or luncheons. Or, as Hadley implied, photo ops. I couldn't imagine

Hadley wearing something like it, even though I had known her only a short time.

"And who might you be?" asked the guard.

Sticking to Big Mike's script, I said, "I'm Annie Chambers. I'm here to see my dad."

The man took out an electronic tablet and pulled up a menu. The name *Chambers* filled his screen. He dialed the number next to the name. My stomach cramped from holding my breath so hard.

Picturing Big Mike or CJ on the other end pretending to be Mr. Chambers—well, I didn't know if it was funny or terrifying. Within a few seconds, the guard was issuing me a badge and directing me to the elevators.

Three people boarded with me, though most were leaving the building. It was almost five o'clock. One man got off on the twenty-first floor, and I exited with him.

We reached the oak double doors to the Caspian Group, Inc., right as a slender woman with buttery yellow hair was leaving. She greeted him warmly as he entered.

"Can I help you?" she asked, blocking my path.

"I'm here looking for someone?" I said.

"Who might that be?" Her tone wasn't exactly inviting.

"Mr. Charles Tillerson." My answer was swift and direct, just the way I had practiced with the PIE Society.

The woman's face looked like it was frozen for just an instant, then she relaxed and smiled.

"Why don't you come inside, Miss…"

"Miss Sly. Jada Sly." No use keeping up the secret-identity bit. I needed Charles to remember me so he could answer my questions about Mama.

Another woman, African American with rich brown skin and jet-black hair, sat behind a reception desk. The buttery-haired woman told her to buzz Mr. Tillerson's office.

I couldn't believe it.

I was in. I was here.

Finally, I was going to get answers.

It seemed to take forever—even though only five minutes had passed—before a short man in a navy suit and lemon-yellow tie rounded the corner and spoke in a soft voice.

"Miss Sly, I am Gavin Gaston. Would you follow me, please?"

I checked my watch. CJ had warned me I had about twenty minutes. I'd already spent at least ten. When I was down to five, Brooklyn was going to send me a text.

I needed to find Charles Tillerson—quickly.

The soft-spoken man led me into a tidy office. When he closed the door, I looked around but didn't see anyone else.

"Where is Charles Tillerson?" I asked. My shoulders were straight, and I was looking directly into his eyes. CJ said important people, especially business types, liked it when a person looked into their eyes.

Mr. Gaston took a moment. He adjusted his tie. He softly drummed his short fingers on the shiny desktop. Then he sighed.

"Mr. Tillerson is no longer here," he said.

"Is he dead?"

"No," Mr. Gaston said after another pause. "He is not dead. But he isn't here, either. What is your business with him, may I ask?"

"Do you know where he is? Did he retire? Where does he live?" I didn't want to babble, but the questions tumbled out. I felt a little frantic.

"You still haven't answered my question. Why are you looking for Mr. Tillerson?"

I opened my mouth to answer, but the phone in my bag buzzed. Before I looked at it, I knew what the message said:

FIVE MINUTES

"Miss? Is everything all right?" Mr. Gaston was now leaning forward. His drumming fingers had gone quiet. Now they pressed against the desktop.

I narrowed my eyes. Too much weirdness was going on. Mama was sneaking around. I was being followed by a guy in a baseball cap; I was mugged by a guy in a hoodie.

I was tired of being pushed around.

Mr. Gaston furrowed his forehead, thick brows nesting in the middle of his face. His voice grew so soft that it raised the hairs on the back of my neck. It was like hearing an animal scurry through the woods but being uncertain where the sound had come from.

"Young lady, I'm going to have to insist. Tell me why you are looking for Mr. Tillerson."

"Because I need answers!" I said.

"What answers?" he said. "Why are you here? I want the truth!"

"You can't HANDLE the truth!" I shouted. I wasn't sure what that meant, but Papa and his brother, my uncle Lou, used to say it back and forth to each other. Then they'd laugh like it was the funniest thing in the world.

Well, it didn't matter. I had no plans to back down. Then Mr. Gaston pressed a button on his phone.

"I need you in here, Dale. Miss Sly is going to be staying with us for a while," he said.

"I'm not staying anywhere!" I said.

When Mr. Gaston stood straighter, I took a step back. I could think of only one thing to do—RUN!

I flipped the chair over, pushed it hard to block him, and threw open the door. The man was yelling, but I kept running.

"Dale! She went that way," he said. I'd turned the corner and was racing past half a dozen closed doors.

An internal alarm sounded. Doors began opening. Mr. Gaston was alerting the people up front not to let me leave.

What was I going to do?

And I didn't even want to think about what would happen if I didn't make it back to the Zoodle Doodle headquarters and meet up with Rainbow and the others.

I remembered CJ saying something about a backup plan, but I had no idea what it was and didn't have time to wonder.

I turned another corner and found myself in a large workroom with a number of desks and mini-walls.

Instantly I dropped to the floor and scampered beneath one desk, then another. The placement of the small walled-off workspaces created a maze. I pressed close to the floor.

Voices moved above and around me.

My heart raced faster.

I pressed tighter against the inside of one of the cubicles.

Three minutes. That was how much time I had left.

I had to get out of this building and back across the street.

I sent a text:

The response was swift:

I put my phone away. Heart pounding in my ears. *Think like a spy. Think like a spy. Think like a spy.*

Deep breath.

My chance finally came when Mr. Gaston trotted past my hiding space toward the front with a few other people. Goodness, I was so scared. This was serious.

I'd thought I'd come here and ask for the man who Mama knew. I wanted to know what he called her about that day. And if it wasn't him, who called about him.

It was important!

Maybe the most important thing ever!

At least, it was for me.

I did not have time for this—playing hide-and-seek with the goon squad!

As soon as Mr. Gaston and his searchers passed,

I headed for the exit. A large metal door was tucked into the far corner of the room. My hand shook just before I pushed it open. *Here's hoping it doesn't set off another alarm.*

I held my breath and pushed.

The stairs stretched forward in two directions—up and down. I practically threw myself down them.

Then I got an idea.

I was still carrying my backpack with my uniform. I ran until I reached the eighteenth floor. Glancing up and down the stairs, I began yanking off the expensive luncheon suit and slipped back into my blouse and jumper. I didn't bother with the stockings.

When I was finally dressed, I stuffed the suit and matching shoes into my bag and hopped out of the stairwell holding my red ballet flats. A woman with a briefcase glanced down and saw me as the elevator door was opening.

"You okay, honey?" she asked.

I rode the rest of the way down, chatting to her. She had round hips and a confident stride. As soon as we hit the lobby, I could see the guards were looking for someone. I pressed close to the woman, like we were together, and did my best to stay out of security's way.

Soon as I hit the street, I was running, running, running.

I was so worried about the guards behind me I almost missed the scene playing out in front of me.

A *whoop-whoop-whoop* alarm was blaring, and the gigantic Zoodle Doodle atop the building spun crazily. A loud recording of a voice drowned out the sound of the people leaving the building.

"Please be advised. We here at Zoodle Doodle have experienced a minor overload. Please relax and let us fix this right away. Have a crispy, zesty Doodle day!"

By the time I reached my SPY pals, they were doubled over with laughter.

"CJ!" Brooklyn sputtered, holding her stomach from laughing. "Dude. Tell your dad or whoever is vice president in charge of Zoodle Doodle's messages that this recording is wack!"

Below her white-blond curtain of hair, the normally cool Hadley gave way to a big smile. "It's a building with a huge cheese puff on the roof. The message, though, is like the cherry on top—or at least the Zoodle. Truly, classic!"

"There you are!" called Rainbow. "I've been looking all over for you."

I smiled sweetly. "I've been in the restroom."

Brooklyn grabbed one arm, Big Mike the other. He said, "Yep, in the ladies' room!"

Of course, he couldn't keep himself from adding, "You know, when my mom is playing the oldies station, she loves this one song from the eighties called 'Meeting in the Ladies Room.' Why do girls like to meet in the—"

"STOP TALKING!" roared Brooklyn, right into his ear.

"Why is that happening?" I asked, referring to the constant whir of the alarm and the repetition of the message blaring from unseen speakers. I was still pretty rattled from my experience across the street, but the fear was turning into a sort of nervous energy.

"Because I pushed the hazard button," CJ said.

"Plan B?" I asked.

He preened, looking quite happy with himself. Then they turned to me. Questions spurted from everyone.

I told them as much as I could before Rainbow and Estelle began herding us across the street.

CJ's nanny, Laura, said, "Mr. Effingham has

arranged for me to accompany all of you down the street for dinner. Follow me, please."

Nervous energy had us all running, squealing, and getting yelled at by our sitters. Now we were laughing hard, mocking each other, and doing anything else to burn off some of the anxiety.

I was reading an e-mail from Cécile saying that Papa had given his okay for me to join the group for dinner when I felt an insistent tug at my arm.

It was Hadley. She slid her gaze to the left, and I followed her look.

"See?" she said in her soft, knowing tone.

"What?" demanded Brooklyn.

"What's going on?" asked CJ and Big Mike together.

Then they all turned. Standing on the street in front of the Braniff Bank Building, as a cold breeze swept off the river and covered me with chills, was a slender man wearing all black. A man we'd all seen before.

Allister Highborne.

What on earth was he doing coming out of the Braniff Bank Building?

CHAPTER 17

My skin crawled when I thought about the soft-spoken man.

Mr. Gaston.

He had given me the creeps.

At school the following day, we were still talking about what had happened at the Zoodle Doodle headquarters and the Braniff Bank Building.

Usually, the International PIE Society met on Tuesdays and Fridays. Thanks to all the events of the previous day—especially the mysterious appearance of Mr. Allister Highborne—an emergency meeting was necessary.

We convinced our usual Wednesday enrichment instructors that we had a pie emergency.

Big Mike said, "I have a surprise for everyone," as soon as we entered the cooking classroom.

However, before he could say another word, there was a knock.

The room was at the far end of our school's main building. No one ever just came down here.

We all stood together and opened the door a crack.

"Hello! Hello! Young people, are you in there?" a voice called.

When we opened the door wider, we saw a small woman in a flowered dress one could only call old-lady chic. Her hair was silver and gray with almost blue highlights.

"Hello," I said. "May we help you?"

"Well," she said in a strong voice, "you are the pie children, am I correct?"

"Yes, ma'am," we said.

With surprising strength, she pushed past us and into the room. She said, "Then I am here to help!"

Her name was Rosemary Grundle. Granny Grundle to her family and friends. She carried a huge bag filled with knitting. She had the biggest feet of any grandmother I'd ever seen. And something about her squared chin and bright eyes felt familiar. Not to mention a mustache, which looked positively itchy.

When she looked at me through her rectangular glasses, I had the strangest feeling that we'd met before. Her pink dress was buttoned right up to her neck.

"I'm replacing your other volunteer. She became ill," said Granny Grundle. "I was applying for the position when the office alerted me that you were having an emergency meeting. A pie emergency, hmm?"

We all looked at one another. Big Mike shrugged. He said, "Uh, yes. A pie emergency." Then his features reddened.

CJ stepped in smoothly, saying, "We had scheduled a pastry chef from La Grenouille to join us for an upcoming, uh, pie-making competition. But she couldn't make it today!"

He said the last part as though it was an utter tragedy of mankind not to have a five-star pastry chef instruct children on baking. Hadley and Big Mike eagerly nodded along.

Big Mike added, "As far as what our chaperone does, well, Mrs. Moldy mostly sat in the chair over there and napped until we needed help."

The woman's face brightened.

"I can definitely do that!" she said. "But first, I'm gonna do my knitting. Carry on, dears!"

We all suffered through a short awkward moment. Soon Granny Grundle was knitting and humming to herself, and we went back to our business. I couldn't help noticing the strong lines converging on her somewhat rectangular features. She caught me looking and I quickly turned away.

Big Mike passed out matching aprons. Each was white with a red-and-white-checked border. A pie-shaped silhouette was stitched up top with the words INTERNATIONAL PIE SOCIETY stitched in black.

"A strong cover story requires good details," he said, showing his lopsided grin. A wild mass of bright red curls swirled around his face.

If strawberry shortcake were human, it would be Big Mike. His cheeks were pink and his skin wore a constellation of tiny freckles. He looked like he was in heaven. I wasn't quite sure whether Big Mike liked spying more than baking.

We all took our monogrammed aprons and tied them on.

"I look cool, even in an apron," CJ said. Hadley gave an eye roll.

We went over the events of the day while Big Mike and Brooklyn removed ingredients from the fridge.

"You like pie making?" I asked Brooklyn. She shrugged.

Big Mike said, "Give it a try, Jada, and you'll be addicted, too!" Then he and Brooklyn argued over the origins of the word *addicted*.

I'd sketched a little when I got home from the restaurant the night before. My drawing was more of a map showing the Zoodle Doodle headquarters and the Braniff Bank Building. Since my journal had been stolen the other day, I'd had to pull out a second journal from Mama. Good thing she had sent me more than one.

"So you think there was something not quite right about the soft-spoken man?" Brooklyn said.

"That guy wasn't all that big, but something about him was creepy!"

"What's our next move?" CJ asked.

"I think the bigger issue right now is Mr. Highborne," Hadley said matter-of-factly. She flicked her blond curtain aside and looked at me. I smiled back.

"She's right," I said. "I don't think it's a coincidence that he was in Lower Manhattan yesterday. We need to know why."

Then an idea hit us all at once. Brooklyn did a stepdance kind of move and gave her bodacious Afro a pat. With two snaps of her fingers that ended in her hands on her hips, she said what all of us were thinking:

"Surveillance time!"

A snort rose up across the room. Granny Grundle let out a long snore. Her knitting needles clanked with each rise and fall of her chest.

"Did you notice the size of her feet?" Brooklyn whispered.

We all glanced in the direction of the sleeping woman. She dozed easily, the pale pink dress with white stripes and a white collar covering her neck. Her feet were up on an ottoman. Big, indeed.

Big Mike kept his voice low. "We need a plan," he said. "How are we going to get the chance to spy on Mr. Highborne?"

The question was still hanging in the air when

the answer knocked at the door. Hadley opened it. This time it was our dean with her hand up, ready to knock again.

Before she could speak, we pointed to our newest volunteer.

Brooklyn said in a low voice, "We just got her down for her nap."

Mrs. Vicario looked as jittery and jumpy as ever. "Good, good," she said, following our lead and whispering. "We were lucky to find another senior volunteer after Mrs. Moldy dropped out so suddenly. I trust you're all doing well with your, uh, club space?"

Her tone was both a question and a statement.

"Yes, ma'am," we said automatically.

The dean went on: "Jada, your grandmother and I have been in touch."

Everyone looked at me. I just shrugged.

"Why is Grandmother Sly staying in touch with you?" I asked.

"Because she wants to ensure you're receiving the highest level of support and education," she said. Her tone indicated that I was silly for even having to ask. Well!

Mrs. Vicario moved on. She said, "When Lady

Sly discovered Jada's interest in our PIE Society, she thought it would be a great idea if we utilized the talents of the group."

We all exchanged glances. I didn't like where this was going.

"And that is why," Mrs. Vicario went on, "she has suggested that you all get practical baking experience. She said her son—Jada, your father—is having a special dinner at the museum to honor the staff and volunteers before the grand reopening."

She clapped her hands together.

The sound echoed.

Granny Grundle sat up instantly. In a gravelly voice, she said, "Is the pie ready, Mother?"

We all stared at her.

She sniffed the air. No pie. A second passed. Then two. We all stood, staring in her direction. Then she cuddled her yarn up to her chin and instantly fell back asleep.

"Well," said Mrs. Vicario. "That was, uh, interesting. As I was saying, Jada, your grandmother had a marvelous suggestion. She wants our very own International PIE Society to work with the staff at the Sly and bake pies for the dinner."

Big Mike broke into a wide grin. "What a great opportunity!" he said. "Your dad has a pastry chef working in the Sly Patisserie who is amazing!"

Mrs. Vicario smiled back at him. She said Grandmother had already arranged for us to work with the pastry staff, who would help us.

After she was gone and Granny Grundle was once again sleeping soundly, CJ said, "Isn't it cool that no one suspects what our real purpose is?"

Brooklyn nodded. "One thing is for sure," she said. "This will be the perfect chance to do some spying."

"Allister Highborne," I said. "We're going to find some answers about him!"

"Yeah, we will!" exclaimed Big Mike.

"Do you think he knows something about your mother's crash?" Brooklyn asked.

I let out a big sigh. "There's something too strange going on with him," I said. "I don't know what Mr. Highborne is up to, but I get a really bad feeling from him."

I couldn't quite figure out whether or not Mr. Highborne had anything to do with Mama.

Something felt off. It had to be more than a

coincidence that I saw him at the Braniff Bank Building, where Mama used to work, on the same day I went there.

It was time for me to find out exactly who I was dealing with!

CHAPTER 18

No more spies. Well, at least no stalkers or followers in dark clothes staring at my ballet studio.

After school the next day, we met at the Sly. Papa and Cécile—not to mention Grandmother—had arranged for us to meet the head baker at the Sly Patisserie. Of course, I'd known her for years. Her name was Miss Honey Bayer, former girl group star of the 1970s.

She was waiting when we arrived.

"Lawd, have mercy on my aching soul!" she exclaimed. Then she let loose a rolling high note that rattled all the pots and pans in the kitchen. She did that sometimes. A chorus of "Oooh, yeah" and "Ooooooooooh, God is good" erupted from her ample bosom like fireworks.

She finally came around an empty sweets case and grabbed me in the best hug ever. When Miss Honey hugged you, you knew you'd been hugged.

"Sugar, just look at you," she went on. "Last time I saw you was when you came home for the holidays two years ago, before your mother passed."

"Yes, ma'am," I said.

After a pause, I turned to introduce her to the others. They were all staring, mouths open.

Miss Honey was as tall as Papa, about six feet. She wore her hair in an old-fashioned beehive that made her look at least a foot taller.

"Everyone, this is the best baker and absolute best singer in the world," I said. "Miss Honey Bayer!"

She took a bow and let loose another string of melodious notes that came straight from her soul.

"Well, look at that. You were always such a solitary girl. I'm glad to see you with some friends now," she said approvingly.

"Miss Honey, they're going to think I am some friendless loser," I said.

She waved her hands. "Oh, poo to that! Bring yourselves on around here. Miss Honey needs to hear 'bout what you plan on cooking up in my kitchen!"

We followed her into the cooking area. Big Mike took one look at her amazing kitchen, and he fell in love.

Then we got down to business. Before any of us could bake, she had a list of rules we needed to follow:

- *No sassing grown folks, even if they in the wrong. ("Tell me and I'll handle them," she said.)*
- *Keep your hands clean.*
- *No running around or shenanigans.*

After that was out of the way, we discussed menu ideas. We talked about whether we would do all baked pies or refrigerator pies or a mix of both. Much as I loved Miss Honey and enjoyed hearing Big Mike's ideas, I was eager to move on to other things.

Even so, Miss Honey demanded to see us in action.

"I've got a reputation, see what I'm saying?" she said, narrowing her eyes at us. "Before anybody serves something outta here, I need to know that they know what they're doing!"

Miss Honey pulled out a recipe that had been handed down from her great-grandmother. Southern-style sweet-potato pie.

"It tastes a lot like pumpkin pie, right?" said Big Mike.

Miss Honey's eyes went wide and rolled back in her head. She began to cough.

"Lawd, have mercy! Child, go on and stab me to death. It would be less painful!" she wailed.

She removed some boiled sweet potatoes from the stovetop. Big Mike, nervous about his mistake, gulped and read carefully through the recipe.

Eggs, cream, butter, nutmeg, cinnamon, salt, vanilla extract, and sugar were gathered. We worked together to measure and blend the ingredients. Miss Honey was right beside us with her two assistants.

In between mixing and adding ingredients, Miss Honey told us about life as a teenage radio superstar.

"Babies, Miss Honey was a showstopper back then," she said. Her wide grin made us smile along with her.

"I tell you the truth," she went on. "Some of

them moves I learned while touring still help me in the kitchen."

Then she aimed a remote at her iPad, and the speakers came to life from music. She did a hip shake and bumped CJ, who went flying across the kitchen.

After that, the rest of us tried some of her moves, and even CJ did his best. I don't think I will ever forget the sight of C. J. Ellis Effingham IV, dressed in crisp khakis and a white polo, trying to imitate the hip swivel of a retired soul singer. Amazing!

Finally, once our sweet-potato pie was out of the oven and ready to cool, we agreed that blueberry, pecan, and sweet potato would be our hot pies, with lemon, banana cream, and chocolate served cold.

Afterward, we tasted the pies and Miss Honey stood over Big Mike and made him declare that sweet-potato pie was superior to pumpkin. We were heading across the lobby that connected the patisserie to the main building when someone cleared his throat.

Mr. Albert Cheswick leaned against his walking stick, with a pipe between his teeth, a twinkle in his eyes, and a smile on his face.

"Good day, Miss Sly," he said. Today he wore a

tiny black hat and wire-rimmed glasses. When he smiled at you, it was hard not to like him. Although, for just a second, I got the strangest feeling.

"Good afternoon, Mr. Cheswick," I said. My gaze continued to trace the shape of his jaw, the angle of his eyes.

"You okay, m'love?" he asked.

I told him I was fine, brushing away the idea that I was seeing something about him today that I hadn't noticed before.

Miss Tutti, who ran the children's parlor at the Sly, told us we had to hold our meeting on the museum's back patio because her storeroom was off-limits for the day.

Well, that made things even better.

It would be a perfect way to keep an eye on Mr. Highborne if he left the building.

I led my fellow secret spies around the museum. We did not see Mr. Highborne in the gift shop or the exhibits or the offices.

Still, I knew another place worth looking into.

The basement.

When I was little, it was my favorite place to play hide-and-seek. To be honest, I did like to go down there and hide because it was impossible for anyone to find me.

Carefully, I opened the door leading to the lower level and beckoned for the others to follow. We stepped around a sign that said DO NOT ENTER.

Automatically, we all bent into a crouch and crept along the dusty corridor leading to the stairs.

"It's very dark," whispered Big Mike.

"Why don't you turn on a flashlight and let Highborne and the whole world know we're here?" CJ said dryly.

"Shhh!" hissed Brooklyn.

Everyone grew quiet again. As we approached the stairs, I signaled left to a barely visible corridor.

There was a space between the ground floor and the basement where a person could hide—uh, I mean, observe.

The space formed a balcony above the basement level. It was too narrow and low for most grown-ups to fit, but I'd always been able to wedge myself into place. Pressing myself flat against the wall, I was still able to squeeze in. So were Hadley and Brooklyn.

However, the boys had a tougher time.

"My head won't fit in there," CJ said. All three of us girls did massive eye rolls.

I whispered to CJ and Big Mike that they should follow the narrow passageway and meet us on the opposite side of the upper area.

"For some reason, you can hear better in that corner," I said, "but because of that beam, you can't see as well."

Hadley added, "CJ, Big Mike, if Highborne comes in and gets any calls, try to hear what he's saying."

"Roger!" said Big Mike.

The boys had moved a few feet when we all heard it.

A distant buzzing sound. Like a phone vibrating. We all looked wide-eyed from one to the other. Slowly, we shook our heads. The buzzing phone wasn't one of ours.

We noticed, however, that Allister Highborne had slid, silent as a shadow, into the room below. He was holding a slim phone to his ear. He began speaking softly.

"Go!" Brooklyn commanded the boys.

CJ and Big Mike scooted along the narrow passageway. The three of us girls squeezed deeper into the shallow overlook and settled into an area that was slightly to the side and back of where Mr. Highborne stood. The entire room below opened up to us, a dim storage area washed over with a palette of grays.

Just like when I was a little kid, it felt as if I was looking down on a dollhouse and could move the pieces wherever I wanted.

"I feel like such an adventurer," Brooklyn said.

"Yes," I agreed. "An archaeologist discovering great mysteries, and of course..."

"Spies saving the world," said Brooklyn.

We shared smiles in the shadows.

Mr. Highborne was gesturing wildly toward the wall in front of him.

This area of the basement held dozens and dozens of boxes. Large cardboard boxes, medium-sized wooden crates. It was storage for items from all over the world and was where extra or unsold merchandise from the museum gift shop was held.

Mr. Highborne skulked along, bent over boxes, ripping them open one at a time.

A sign on the wall read STORAGE FOR GIFT SHOP.

He held a small box cutter. Its sharp, pointy blade glinted in the dim lighting. Mr. Highborne didn't turn on any lights. He moved quickly. His frustration showed each time he stabbed a box with the blade, rummaged inside, and didn't find what he was looking for.

Was he searching for something to steal?

Or was he up to something else?

Some items in the museum store could be pretty expensive replicas of original works of art. Was he merely a crook? Or was there more to it than that?

That thought gave me an idea.

"Girls," I whispered. We knelt below the upper wall in case he caught a vibration and looked up. "We need to talk to someone in the gift shop."

Brooklyn was nodding already. "I was thinking the exact same thing!" she said.

When we lifted our heads for another peek, we saw that Mr. Highborne had paused. He released a deep sigh.

The wall he was staring at was filled with stacks and stacks of boxes. I could see red leather-bound journals in the open ones. Official Sly Museum art journals like the ones Mama had sent to me.

Carefully, he removed a journal, touched all the pages slowly, turned it over, then moved on to the next.

It was like the night I'd met him here. Why was he obsessed with the journals?

Hadley did a slow head turn and stared at me. "You said someone shoved you and took your sketchbook, right?" she asked. "Could it have been him?"

I shook my head. I didn't like the man, but I knew he wasn't the one who'd stole from me.

"No," I said. "The guy who took my sketchbook was even thinner and younger. Not a teenager but, like, in college, maybe."

"And not the same man who followed you to your dance class, and that other time on the subway?" Brooklyn pressed.

I shook my head. "The guy from the subway with the baseball cap was short, not much taller than us. Kind of built. You know? Square," I said.

Brooklyn nodded.

I scooted back, slowly, slowly, slowly. When I finally reached the little step down, dust bunnies stuck to me and clung to Brooklyn's Afro. I brushed at the ones on my clothes and her hair. A silent flurry of dust formed a blizzard around me.

"Hu-hu-hu…" I huffed while trying to make as little noise as possible. The sneeze was building, building, building. It tickled all the way back into my brain.

The three of us froze.

Brooklyn jabbed her finger flat beneath my nose. She shook her head at me. Her brows squeezed fiercely together. She shook her head again, slowly, never taking her eyes off mine. Was she trying to hypnotize me?

Whatever it was, it worked.

The sneeze evaporated in my nose. I drew a shallow, shaky breath.

As quietly as possible, we moved down to the lower floor.

Now Mr. Highborne was only a few feet away. The whine of distant power saws vibrated through the stone floors. Construction workers laughed amid the grind and whir of mechanical noises on the first floor. I crept closer and closer to Highborne.

Quietly, I said, "Excuse me, what are you looking for?"

"AHHHHHH!" Allister screamed.

Until that moment, I didn't think I'd ever heard a grown man scream.

"What on earth? What? What?" He was stammering, his milk-white cheeks stained a vicious red.

"Are you mad?" he said after a moment. He had stepped away from me. His icy blue eyes remained wild with fright.

He made himself stand up straight and tall. Ran a hand through his swept-over bangs.

He puffed himself up, saying, "What are you girls doing down here? Can't you read? The museum is closed and this area is off-limits. There are signs all over."

I gave a little sniff, not at all enjoying his attitude.

"Papa told me my friends and I could look around today," I fudged. "As for this basement being off-limits, well, I guess we didn't see the sign."

I smiled sweetly. For sure, it was insincere, but I tried to make it appear otherwise.

He narrowed his eyes—clearly my acting skills needed improvement. I narrowed my eyes, as well.

"Does your father know you're down here snooping around?" he asked, crossing his arms.

"Does he know *you're* down here snooping around?" I said—sweetly, of course.

My hands moved to my hips. I was getting irritated. Then I realized something: This must have been exactly where he was coming from when the alarm was going off and the police were here.

Beyond where he stood, I could make out box after box. These were stamped OVERSTOCK INVENTORY for the gift shop.

The boxes must have been full of old sketchbook journals. I thought about what he'd said that first day we met, about my journal being the new style. But the ones he was going through were the old familiar design.

Brooklyn said, "Hi, um, we just wanted to know why you're so interested in the sketchbooks? I mean, they're available in the museum gift shop, right? So, why—"

She didn't get to finish her question, because a voice was calling from the stairs.

It was Cécile.

"Jada? Jada, are you down there?" she asked in her French accent.

I turned to find her putting on her coat. Cécile looked at Hadley and Brooklyn and said, "Oh, hello, girls. Jada, please get your things. We have to go."

She said good evening to Mr. Highborne, then helped me into my peacoat. "We have to leave. Your father needs to see you."

That didn't sound good.

Brooklyn and Hadley said good-bye, and we all began climbing the steps to the main floor. I looked back to find Mr. Highborne staring at me.

It was so weird. He looked more concerned than angry.

Why on earth would he be concerned?

Maybe because we were getting too close to the truth.

Cécile was quiet most of the train ride home. By the time we reached the brownstone, I had a knot the size of the Statue of Liberty in my stomach. We entered through the kitchen door. Cold air left my cheeks cool and blotchy. Cécile gave me a nudge into the living room.

Papa had his back to the kitchen. When I entered the room, he turned.

Then I noticed a man I'd never seen before. That only made me more curious.

But when I saw the third man in the room, my curiosity turned to cold, hard dread.

It was the soft-spoken Mr. Gaston.

Standing in my living room!

CHAPTER 19

Mr. Gaston and the other man stood as we entered the room.

"What is all this?" I said. My gaze swept from the stranger and Mr. Gaston to Papa. Papa looked angry. Even so, he had on his concerned-parent face.

Not good.

"Jada, please come sit over here," Papa said. He guided me to a seat beside his chair. I sat there, looking from face to face, and the two men took seats, too. My knees were trembling so hard that my cat socks looked as if they might run.

I wanted more than anything to be in my bedroom on my bed with Josephine Baker.

Papa let out a great heavy sigh. He said, "Is it true, Jada? Mr. Gaston says when you were supposed to be with your schoolmates touring the Zoodle Doodle headquarters, you were instead in his office asking questions about your mother?"

"I..." The lump in my throat dissolved into a bitter taste. "Papa, I was asking about someone who worked with Mama, that's all!"

"Jada! What were you thinking? That was so dangerous, slipping away from Rainbow. Why would you do this?"

My eyes went from him to the stranger to Mr. Gaston. I drew a deep breath and tried to explain.

"Papa, please. It's just that I have this feeling—"

But he was already shaking his head. He cut in before I could finish.

"Jada, darling, we talked about this back in Bordeaux. Baby, I think it's time we talked about it again," he said.

It was like needles poking me from my feet to my head. I felt my cheeks getting red.

"I want you to meet someone." He turned to the

man seated on his opposite side. "This is Dr. Gerard. He's a well-respected psychologist—"

"No! No! No!" I shouted, springing to my feet.

"Jada, please." Papa pulled at my hand.

"What did this man tell you? What did he say?" I said. I was stabbing my finger toward Mr. Gaston.

Papa pulled me back into my seat and clasped my hands.

"Mr. Gaston told me about your visit. Jada, you promised you weren't spying anymore." Papa was trying to sound supportive. "You promised, Jada. And the minute I give you some freedom, what do you do?"

"But—"

"No, Jada. What did you do?"

Tears stung my eyes, but I refused to cry in front of any of them.

"You don't understand!" I managed to say.

Dr. Gerard took over. He slid closer to me. "Jada—may I call you that?"

His soothing tone and sweater-vest made him look professor-ish.

"Papa!" I cried out, twisting in my seat to find

him across the room, running his fingers through his tangle of curls.

"Jada…" Papa said. He sounded tired.

A sick feeling bubbled in my stomach.

My emotions were building. I'd been keeping them all locked away because I knew Papa didn't want to know how I really felt.

Now everything was falling apart.

Maybe if I'd shared my sketchbook with Papa and shown him my notes. Maybe he would've understood I needed answers.

Mr. Gaston stood. He said to my father, "I am so sorry for this, Dr. Sly. Out of respect for you and your late wife, I thought you should know. We were just so concerned about her the other day."

"If you were so concerned, why'd you wait two days before coming over here?" I shouted.

"Jada! Lower your voice. You will NOT be disrespectful to adults in our home!" Papa said.

Mr. Gaston was such a little liar face.

What about how intense he got in his office—how he commanded me to tell him the real reason I was there?

"Dr. Sly," Mr. Gaston said, his voice low and even, "I will leave you to handle this matter. I am so sorry to have troubled your family."

"Where is Charles Tillerson?" The question popped out of me before I could think about it.

Mr. Gaston appeared to flinch at the mention of the man's name.

He took a second to compose himself and said, "Mr. Tillerson retired years ago."

"Then why not say that in your office? Can you answer that one simple question? All I wanted was an answer!"

When I looked at Mr. Gaston, I was sure for a moment I saw a slight tic at the corner of his eye.

He slipped into his topcoat. Now he looked calm. Coolheaded. Not at all like a man who'd tried to capture a girl at his office a few days ago.

"I'm sorry if I caused you any distress, Miss Sly," he said.

Papa walked Mr. Gaston to the door. They spoke in hushed tones, but I was certain Papa was apologizing for my behavior.

When he returned, I was so worked up I could barely breathe.

"Jada, I want you to go to your room now," Papa said.

"Papa, please, give me a chance to explain my side," I said.

"What side?" he exploded.

Dr. Gerard stood. "Dr. Sly, Ben, I think Jada deserves time to process this," he said. Then he turned to me and went on. "You're grieving, and that's okay."

"I am not grieving! I am not processing anything. I'm trying to tell you that Mama did not die in that stupid crash!"

Now tears poked at my eyes and began to tumble down my cheeks.

Papa let out a long sigh. This time he pulled me into his arms.

Since Mama's plane crashed, I'd been holding back all the fear, pain, and everything that comes when someone you love could be gone for good. All my strength, that belief, was dissolving, breaking away.

"She is alive," I sobbed, pushing away from Papa. "She is alive."

Papa reached for me again. I slapped away his hand.

"No, I'm not making it up. I've seen her multiple times," I said. "She was just in Central Park."

He and Dr. Gerard looked at each other.

"I AM SERIOUS!" I screamed.

"Jada, you feel frustrated, don't you?" Dr. Gerard said. I just stood, glaring at him, his image blurred through my tears.

He went on. "What if I could help you figure out what was really going on? Your dad tells me you love spying. You and your mother played spy games all the time, right?"

I nodded, but kept my arms crossed tightly over my body even as the tears flowed.

"Well," he said in his calm tone, "what if I could help you with your investigation? But maybe we could come at it from a slightly different approach. Would that be okay?"

I swallowed hard.

"I guess," I said.

Dr. Gerard said he thought I should go lie down and plan to see him in his office the next day. I agreed. When Papa tried to give me another hug, I pushed him away.

Why was he so willing to believe everyone but me?

In my room I sobbed freely. Josephine licked my fingers, and I scooped her up and hugged her to my chest.

Even as the misery of what had just happened sent shudders through my whole body, one question whispered to the far corners of my brain:

Mr. Gaston looked really nervous when I mentioned Charles Tillerson.

Why?

CHAPTER 20

Grief was a lot like being alone on an island.

If people squint, they can see you—but they can't *really* see you.

Oh, for goodness' sake! I was a spy who had information to gather and minds to change! No time for poetry.

Papa kept me home from school on Friday. I think Rainbow retired from the nanny business after Papa told her about me sneaking into the Braniff Bank Building. I stayed in my bedroom. The house-keeper brought up some of my favorite breakfast foods—yogurt, croissants, marmalade, and fresh fruits.

I wasn't hungry.

Food wasn't what I wanted, but I needed it to keep up my strength. I was a strong, resourceful spy. Resolute and everything!

I took a huge bite of an apple.

Even though I'd been quarantined like I had a disease, it didn't stop me from texting my friends and telling them what had happened. I told them how Papa had insisted I stay home and "rest." Who was I? Granny Grundle?

At first their utter outrage made me happy. They flooded my phone with words of support.

Then I realized all of it was frustrating, as Dr. Gerard had said. I felt so tired. So I slept.

Hours later, I awoke with bed head and a dry mouth. A wedge of apple clung to my lip. I swept it away.

My eyes felt grainy. A bottle of water sat by the bed. I drank it all down in one long gulp.

I remembered what I'd been dreaming. It had been about Mr. Charles Tillerson. I'd been able to see him clear as anything. But he kept changing into someone else. Someone I couldn't quite make out. He looked different, but his voice. There was something about his voice.

I'd been so young when I met him, I really didn't remember much—shorter than Mama, black hair with a lot of silver on the sides, regular build. I didn't appreciate personal geometry back then, so I knew almost nothing about the lines and planes of his face.

But there was something else, too.

I just couldn't remember what!

My sketchbook was tucked away in my desk drawer. I took it out and brought it to my bed. Josephine Baker was hopping around her play area. I scooped her up and brought her to my bed, too.

I'd been sketching, trying to record as much as I could remember from my journal that was taken.

I stared at all my evidence. I'd always trusted myself. Sure, I knew I liked to fantasize dangerous missions a lot. But I always knew the difference between reality and imagination.

Now, staring at the sketchbook, I felt like maybe I was beginning to mix the two.

It was just that I was so sure Mama had been a real spy.

And I was positive I'd seen her in Central Park

and other places since arriving in New York City. That felt real to me.

But the idea of not being able to believe in myself gave me a shudder.

A light knock at my bedroom door was followed by a head poking around the corner. Cécile.

"Ah, Jada, did I awaken you?" she asked.

"No," I said, my voice steady.

She came over to the bed, cupped my face in her hands, and smiled. "Do not worry, *ma chérie*. It will get better."

My attempt at being strong crumbled. I grabbed her around the waist.

"Promise?"

She lightly batted the tip of my nose. "Promise."

Even though I'd been working hard to get Papa to believe Mama was alive before he could fall in love with Cécile, I loved her. She had always been a good friend to me. To us.

I cuddled up next to her and my bunny rabbit, closing the book on my thoughts. Papa had made an appointment with Dr. Gerard for this afternoon. There was no getting out of it.

Not now. Not with everything that had happened.

The hour I spent with Dr. Gerard wasn't a total waste—the man did know how to listen. He didn't force me to talk about Mama or anything. We mostly talked about my sketches. I wasn't sure why, but I'd taken my sketchbook with me. I spent most of the time drawing him while he chatted about how the mind works and "the five stages of grief."

Apparently, I was stuck in the first two stages—denial and anger. If I could get myself together, the next stage I had to look forward to was bargaining—saying all the things I'd do if only Mama would come back.

It sounded ridiculous.

But maybe it wasn't so far-fetched.

I would have given anything to prove she *wasn't* dead!

By the time the session ended, I felt like I didn't hate it as much as I'd imagined I would. But I needed more time to think.

Papa and Cécile sat across from me at Alice's Tea Cup. Apparently the best way to follow up a session with a therapist was with tea and delicious, buttery scones in a lovely Upper West Side eatery.

The smell of butter, cakes, ham, and cheese wafted through the air. Babies in strollers giggled or stared at the fairy-tale painted ceiling. It had always been one of my favorite places.

Cécile smiled at me. "How do you like the tea?" she asked for perhaps the third time. She was only making small talk. No doubt Dr. Gerard must have some kind of rule about not badgering the patient. Papa had asked only once. When I'd remained silent, the two of them began an endless stream of upbeat chitchat.

We used to come here a lot before we moved. Me, Papa, and Mama. Even afterward, when we'd come back to New York for visits, Mama made a point of bringing us. A family tradition, she'd said.

Now I looked across the table, observing how comfortable the two of them were with each other.

"Are you two a…a couple now?" I asked. My throat felt dry. My eyes began to burn. The flaky crust of the scone felt gummy in my stomach.

I'd been watching them—the little light touches, the easy way they laughed together, the way Papa turned to her or blushed ever so slightly when she looked at him.

It was like watching him with Mama, only Mama wasn't here anymore.

"Jada, I—" Papa began.

"We…" said Cécile. The two of them stammered over their words, looked back and forth between one another.

And I knew I wasn't wrong.

For a brief moment, a surge of the same white-hot anger from the night before rose into my chest, burning like lava.

I pushed away my plate, unable to finish my food.

"It's not like that," Papa said. "We're not a couple, well, not exactly. But I care for Cécile. A lot."

"We would never do anything to hurt you," Cécile said. Her eyes were sad. She'd always seemed like such a friend to me.

I slid out of the booth. "I need some time alone, and fresh air. I'm walking home. By myself," I said.

Papa stood so abruptly he knocked his chair onto the wooden floor.

"Don't be absurd. You'll do no such thing. It's going to be dark soon," he said.

"LEAVE ME ALONE!" I shouted. The restaurant went silent. A balloon popped somewhere, and a baby began to wail. I raced from the room, yelling, "Don't follow me! Don't follow me!"

Cold autumn air slapped at my face and stung against my hot tears. I clutched my sketchbook, slung my backpack over one shoulder, and ran as fast as I could.

When I finally stopped, I spun wildly, expecting to see Papa and Cécile hot on my trail. They weren't. I realized I was getting out of control. This wasn't me. All the crying and anger and uncertainty.

It wasn't the real me.

Our brownstone was only a few blocks away. Why couldn't he have let me have a few moments to myself? Why'd he have to make such a big deal out of it?

Enormous shadows began to overpower everyone on the sidewalk. Daylight was draining away, and the tall buildings blocked out much of the remaining sunlight.

My pace quickened with my heart rate. I huddled into my jacket and pulled my backpack tighter.

Only a block to go.

My cheeks were getting cold, and so were my fingers. I had my own key, and the housekeeper was there.

I'd turned onto my street when I heard a car backfire. I looked up just in time to see a man duck behind a truck. The same size and build as the man in the baseball cap I'd spotted following us in the subway.

Was I being followed again?

Or were all these sightings another part of my "process"?

Was he there—or was my grief making me see things that weren't there at all?

One way to find out.

I was across the street. When the traffic cleared and I crossed, rather than turn down the sidewalk that led to our kitchen door, I kept walking.

Then I was running, hard as I could.

A thousand feelings crammed into my head all at once, making me dizzy. I'd been unsure if I could trust myself. Unsure of what to think or how to feel.

Then I saw him.

The same man.

He hit the intersection running. I ran across the street, then ducked behind some bushes beside a church.

I allowed myself a little smile.

Because I could see him.

Dr. Gerard had spent some time trying to help me understand why I might need to invent intrigue as a way of coping with Mama's death.

But I hadn't imagined the man in the baseball cap. He was right here. I squelched the urge to raise my arms in triumph and yell, "Aha!"

A distant sound like wind chimes rattled. The wind was picking up, and the sky was turning from purple to midnight blue. Papa and Cécile would be home soon. If I wasn't there when they arrived, I might find myself in big trouble.

Turning from my hiding place and brushing leaves off my jacket, I heard tires squeal. I froze. The car was in the intersection. The man who'd been following me yanked open the door, got inside, and slammed the door closed. The car began to creep away.

I took a step toward the street. Allister Highborne was driving the car. He had picked up the man in the baseball cap.

What on earth did the two of them have in common?

I gulped.

ME!

Anger welled up inside me, and I was about to race toward the street where the car continued to slowly drive away—no doubt wondering where I was hiding. I was ready to take off when a hand reached out, grabbed me, and spun me around.

I readied myself to drop into a fighting stance.

But I could not have prepared for the face looking down into mine.

"Hello, Jada!"

Mama!

It was really her!

CHAPTER 21

"Mama!" I said it in a whisper. If I spoke too loudly, I feared she'd disappear again.

She dropped down to her knees and pulled me to her. She hugged me hard, and when she released me, I wasn't ready to let go.

"You *are* alive! I knew it! I knew it!"

"Shhh, shhh, shhh, baby," she said. She laid her finger on my lips. Her gaze softened, and her mouth curled into a tiny smile. "It is so very good to finally hold you in my arms again. And look at your hair. You're so grown-up!"

A car door slammed in the distance, making us both tense up. Mama hugged me again, this time protectively. When she pulled back enough to look at me, the smile was gone.

"Jada, listen to me—we don't have much time," she said.

The wind rose, and October leaves skittered across the pavement. A chill started deep inside me.

Mama's dark eyes blazed. She stared with such intensity that it gave off heat.

"What's wrong, Mama? Why won't you come home? What are you hiding from? Who is Charles Tillerson?"

"Jada!" She gave me a gentle yet firm shake. She pulled me even closer and placed her lips beside my ear. "We don't have much time," she repeated. "You have to stop searching for me. I've been trying to watch out for your safety. But my safety depends on people believing I'm dead."

She paused, drawing a breath before continuing.

"It's been hard. I let myself get too close. I didn't mean for you to spot me in Central Park."

"But, Mama, you're the one who taught me to spot when someone was watching," I said.

"Besides, Central Park wasn't the first time I spotted you!"

She gave a little laugh. "I think I taught you too well."

A dog barked down the block. Then voices. People were walking toward us on the sidewalk.

It was Papa and Cécile!

Mama turned sharply toward the voices. She tugged me deeper into the bushes lining the church walkway. We both listened for a second. My heart was racing so hard I could barely hear anything else.

Mama's whisper was insistent.

"Baby, I know you want answers. I promise, soon as I can, I will give them to you. But listen to me— stay away from the Braniff Bank Building and forget Charles Tillerson."

"You wrote his name on the back of that postcard. Why?"

Now the voices were close enough to hear.

"…is having a hard time. You must give her time, Benjamin. She is a beautiful, bright child. She will eventually accept that which she cannot deny."

The voice belonged to Cécile. Mama and I exchanged glances.

My whisper grew urgent. "Mama! If you don't come home soon, Papa is going to fall in love with Cécile. It's already started to happen. You have to come home. Let me help you!"

She hugged me to her.

"I'm not completely alone. I do have some help. But the situation is so unstable I can't risk staying in contact with the people on my side."

"Who is helping you?" I really needed to know.

But Mama clearly believed the less I knew the better.

"Jada, now listen to me. No one—*No one*—must know you saw me. Do not tell your father," she said. "Can you do that? Promise me!"

"But Mama—"

"Listen. This is not a game like we used to play. Bad people out there would do anything to get their hands on—"

"Jada! Jada!" Papa's voice bounced off the wind. He and Cécile must've gone inside already and realized I wasn't upstairs.

"You'd better go!" Mama said.

"NO! I don't want to go. I don't want you to go." I was being stubborn and willful, but the idea of letting go of her was tearing my heart apart.

"Come this way!" Mama said.

She grabbed my wrist and tugged me into a narrow alleyway behind the church. Mama placed her finger on her lips, signaling for me to be silent.

We moved quickly down the walkway until we stood directly behind the rear gate of the Sly brownstone.

"You get inside and be safe," Mama said. She tried to nudge me forward, but I dug my heels in— literally.

"Mama, if you don't come home now, you might not be able to. Papa is falling in love with Cécile. We need you. I need you." Nothing was going the way I'd pictured it. Mama was supposed to come home when I found her.

"Jada!" Her voice was right next to my ear. "Your father and Cécile deserve to be happy. I promise I will explain everything. Right now I'm safe because bad people I once trusted think I am dead. I need to keep it that way!"

"What are they looking for?" I asked. I was stalling, doing whatever I could to keep Mama with me a few moments longer.

"I trusted the wrong people, Jada. I found

something—something valuable—and turned it in to the wrong person."

Something valuable?

"You mean like diamonds! Gold! A treasure!"

She smiled, but it was sad and made me feel lonely in my heart.

"No, baby," she said, absently brushing my hair out of my face. "Not that kind of value. In my world, nothing is as valuable as information. What I found could have put a lot of important people in jeopardy. The person I trusted betrayed me. Only he didn't know I kept a copy."

Papa's voice rose above the wind.

"Jada Marie! If you're out here, please come inside," he said.

"You have to go. So do I," Mama said.

"Mama, wait! What is it? What did you copy?" Anger, frustration, and fear jumbled inside me.

"I'm afraid your mama got a little too clever for her own good. I hid the proof so well that…um, it got lost. Now we're having trouble finding it. The others know, so they're desperate to get to it first."

She was pulling away from me. I could feel her vanishing right before my eyes.

In a hushed tone, she said, "Just remember what I said—no one can know we talked. And, baby, whatever you do, stop looking for Charles Tillerson. Finding him would be dangerous—for both of us!"

Papa called out to me again. I turned toward his voice. Confusion weighed on me like chains.

"Mama..."

She was gone.

My heart thudded in my chest. The alley was deserted. Darkness came alive with critters scampering.

Papa called my name yet again. I pushed open the rear gate, moving toward the kitchen door.

My whole body felt numb. I'd been working so hard to figure out where Mama was and why. Then, out of nowhere, she appeared. But finding her had not gone like I'd thought it would.

When I moved beyond the back garden into the light of the outdoor security lamp, Papa ran down the steps. I expected him to be angry and start shouting at me again.

Instead, just like Mama had done, he pulled me into a hug. This time I did not push away.

Even so, I couldn't feel his warmth.

Seeing Mama had left me too numb.

And too afraid.

What if she had no intention of coming back home with Papa and me?

Hours later, I stood at my bedroom window and stared down at the backyard. I knew it was crazy, but I kept looking at the spot where Mama and I had been, beyond the rear gate. I stared and stared, hoping she'd come back.

She did not.

Fear made me weak-kneed. After a while, however, fear was replaced by something else:

Resolve.

My heart thundered, but my brain was finding its own rhythm.

Mama had demanded that I stay away from Mr. Tillerson. I gritted my teeth.

I couldn't. I couldn't stay away.

Charles Tillerson was the key to everything.

Moonlight dappled the ground. The backyard was motionless. Now my hands rested on my hips.

I was going to find Charles Tillerson.

Mama needed protecting. She needed my help.

And she was going to get my help, whether she liked it or not!

CHAPTER 22

On Saturday, the PIE Society met at the kitchen of the patisserie. Miss Honey greeted us with her warm smile and reminded us that if anyone forgot her rules, she'd toss them outside with the garbage!

Then she sang a three-song medley of her biggest hits from her former girl band—the Sensations!

Miss Honey invited us to work on our desserts. Everyone was there except CJ. He was getting a private tour of the US Mint, probably creating a coin with his face on it.

I felt like I was being held underwater. Everyone

around me seemed distorted. If Papa had asked me to compare how I felt to a famous painter's work, it would have to be Salvador Dalí's. His pictures were weird and sometimes even scary. Exactly what I was feeling.

A full day had gone by since I discovered Mama was alive.

I had talked to her, hugged her.

Then I'd had to let her go!

It wasn't fair.

Big Mike was saying, "I've been hearing radio ads and seeing stuff all over the place about the Sly's big reopening."

Unable to help himself, he went into one of his did-you-know explanations about how museums originated in the nineteenth century in South America. He grinned wide until Brooklyn shot back with her own facts.

She said, "Uh-uh-uh. In 1683 the world's first university museum opened in Oxford, England. The Ashmolean Museum housed the collections of Elias Ashmole! HA!"

An evil look of glee flitted across her face. As out of sorts as I felt, I almost smiled. Then Brooklyn burst out laughing and grabbed Big Mike.

"I'm just messing with you—even though I am one hundred percent right," she said. She gave him a playful shove, and he grinned.

"Well, there is this one thing I learned about pies…" he began.

We all groaned.

Brooklyn looked at me, hard.

"You don't look so good, Parlez-Vous. What's up?" she said.

I could feel Hadley watching me, too. Big Mike was on his tablet, no doubt double-checking Brooklyn's museum facts.

"Are you still down about your daddy making you stay home yesterday?" Brooklyn asked.

I drew in a big breath.

Mama had been very clear—no one was to know that I'd seen her. Even so, I couldn't help feeling she was still in real trouble. If I didn't do something to help, I might never see her again.

"I'm all right," I said, taking another big breath. "I still can't believe Mr. Gaston from the Braniff Bank Building showed up at our house!"

"And tattled!" said Hadley. "Grown-ups who tattle are the worst! He had a lot of nerve!"

"I'll bet Mr. Soft Voice didn't tell your father how he and his goons tried to capture you."

"No, he did not," I said, shaking my head.

Not being able to tell the whole truth made me feel jittery. But it couldn't be helped. Still, being around my friends made me feel calmer.

Now for the next part.

Another deep breath.

I told them my thoughts about Mr. Highborne and the man with the baseball cap, a.k.a. my subway stalker.

"We have got to find out who this dude really is, right? Highborne, I mean," Brooklyn said.

"The baseball cap guy, too," Hadley said, sounding bored but looking totally alert.

All three of them were staring at me. Their expressions were so serious and sincere I wanted to hug each of them.

I understood why Mama wanted to stay in hiding—bad people thought she was dead, so she wasn't a threat. If she let herself get seen or if I blabbed, they would know she was alive and they'd be after her again.

If only she had told me what she was trying to find.

Still, I hadn't had a chance to tell her about any of

the drama going on around here. Such as Mr. High-borne and his connection to a man who'd been following me.

Big Mike grabbed my sketchbook and pencil. Turned to a clean page and went to work.

"Okay, let's walk through this," he said. Then he proceeded to draw a diagram based on my notes:

- Subway stalker...short man with a squarish head beneath a baseball cap
- Airport/subway mugger...long and thin, shaped like a rectangle
- Allister Highborne...Jada's father's assistant, wears a turtleneck (A crime in itself, I think.)

Big Mike drew a line from Baseball Cap to Highborne. He said, "Now, we know the two of them are somehow connected—oh, wait."

He went back to his list. His eyes wore a soft expression when he looked at me and wrote *Jada's mom*. I bit the inside corner of my lip to hide the wide grin pushing across my face.

Big Mike seemed to sense I needed a break. Putting away his diagram, we returned to our kitchen duties. Miss Honey had gone to check on something. I did not want her to catch us solving a mystery when there was work to be done.

We rolled dough and pounded butter and lard together until our hands ached.

"The dinner is next Thursday," Miss Honey was saying while Hadley rolled a small piece of dough over and over like Play-Doh. "We have about thirty people coming here to celebrate everybody's hard work for the reopening."

She put her hands on her hips and then gave each of us a good long look. When she looked at me, she showed a wide grin and clapped her plump hands together, sending a cloud of powdered sugar floating around us.

I wondered if Papa had told her about my recent, uh, troubles when she gave me a nod and a wink.

Miss Honey became all business, giving us a stern look.

"You children have been real sweethearts so far, but next week you need to show up with your game faces on, ready to work, you see what I'm saying? Some weepy-sounding woman named Bacarro or Bacarrio—"

"Mrs. Vicario," Big Mike said. Miss Honey cut her eyes to him, and he quickly added, "Not that it matters."

"Well, whatever," the baker said, "she called and said next Thursday she's letting y'all out early so long as your parents sign a permission slip. Said she'll give it to you herself on Monday. Get those papers signed. I'll need you here around three. Don't. Be. Late!"

I had the urge to salute.

She smiled at us and pulled us all into a group hug. "Awwww, good children. Such good children. Now go on and get outta my kitchen. I've got work to do!" Then she sang, "Do-do-do, OWWWWWW!" That last, piercing note caused us all to jump, and we raced out of the kitchen. Thank goodness for the double-paned glass in the window, saving it from breaking from the sound.

"No running, you hear me?" she shouted behind us.

We left the patisserie and headed for our old meeting spot in the storeroom.

Once we were safely hidden, I pulled out my sketchbook, and we went over all the information we'd gathered.

"What are you going to do about Charles Tillerson?" Hadley asked.

I'd noticed that her voice became less whispery the more time we spent together. She was quiet, but fierce. I liked how she studied things and took her time, unlike Brooklyn or Big Mike. I loved them, too, though.

That hit me.

I loved them. I loved all of them. Even CJ. In a very short time, we'd grown close. Being a spy would have been way less enjoyable without them.

"The other day, before I was so rudely taken away," I said, "I had an idea. We need to talk to the people in charge of the museum shop. We need to understand more about the journals."

"Especially the ones creepy Highborne can't seem to stop staring at," Brooklyn said.

Our fact-finding mission to the museum store didn't tell us a whole lot. A girl I didn't know was inside unpacking boxes. She said she'd been hired to help get the store up and running again.

"Those sketchbooks in the basement are the old design," she said in a nasally, I-don't-want-to-be-bothered tone. She had eight tiny hoops in one ear, nine in the other. Thick black lines were etched beneath her brown eyes.

"I don't know why those sketchbooks are down

there. Someone ordered a whole new design. I'm told they'd just gotten a few prototypes when the museum decided to shut down for its remodel," she said.

Big Mike asked, "What's the difference between the old style and the new ones?"

She gave another big sigh and said the new style had thicker paper. And of course, the new ones were embossed with a new logo.

We went back to our meeting spot.

I'd hoped to learn more.

Big Mike said, "Even though we don't know much, we do know those sketchbooks seem to somehow be involved with Jada, the man from the subway, and Mr. Highborne."

"We need to figure out why Baseball Cap, a.k.a. Subway Stalker, is following you," Brooklyn said.

"Can we please give him one name or the other?" Hadley asked.

We all turned and stared at her. She held her arms open. Her visible eyebrow shot upward.

"What? It's confusing, that's all," she said.

We all looked at one another. Big Mike shrugged and I nodded at him. He said, "Baseball Cap. From now on, we'll refer to the guy who keeps showing up in the subway and in front of buildings and now in a car driven by Highborne as Baseball Cap."

That drew nods of approval. Then Hadley had a question: "What if he isn't following you?"

"Explain, please," Brooklyn said.

"Well, what if this has something to do with the museum?" she said.

Big Mike frowned, then his cheeks turned bright pink. "Yeah, Jada. Think about it. You said Highborne was in charge here before your dad came back. Maybe he liked it. Maybe he doesn't want to give up being a director or whatever," he said.

I nodded. Hadley pointed at the tiny window in the rear of the room.

Allister Highborne was heading down Central Park West. It was now or never. The perfect time to follow him. We needed to know what he was up to!

Luckily for us, the parlor was empty. We dashed down a back hallway to a side door. We pushed it with such force that it banged. I was certain he heard.

We stood, frozen, waiting for him to turn back. But he kept walking.

Brooklyn directed us to cross the street. "It'll be easier to blend with people in the park," she said.

Cooler temperatures were leading to more and more color changes among the leaves. Deep reds and bright golds dangled like fabulous flags. We slipped quietly up the sidewalk wrapped comfortably in leafy shade.

He stopped abruptly, his hand fishing around in his pocket.

A few seconds later, he was heading back toward the museum.

"Go, go, go!" I whispered.

We raced toward 110th Street, getting there just in time to mix with the flow of pedestrians crossing the street. By the time Mr. Highborne reached the intersection on his side of the street, we were pushing our way through the front door.

For some reason, we all ducked down as we entered.

When we reached the lobby, Hadley tugged at my sleeve. "Brooklyn said we could access his e-mail if we cloned his phone," she said.

I frowned. "Clone a phone? I don't even know what that means."

"I do. Show me his office," she said. "Then create a distraction."

So that was what we did.

Brooklyn, Big Mike, and I caught up with Mr. Highborne.

"What brings you to the administrative floor?" he said. No hello at all. Just his usual smug smugness!

"Good morning, Mr. Highborne," I said. My sweet smile was firmly in place. "You remember my good friends Brooklyn and Big Mike, don't you?"

"You know your dad had to step out. He's not here right now," he said, looking from me to Brooklyn to Big Mike and back to me. Of course I knew Papa was gone.

"Oh, darn!" I said. "I thought he was still around."

We wanted to lead him away from his doorway. I kept taking tiny steps backward. Hadley had disappeared.

"Well, it's been nice chatting, but I left my phone in my office and I need to go. Grown-up stuff to do, places to be, and all that," he said. He was very snarky.

All of a sudden, he spun around, and my heart nearly jumped out of my throat. Standing right behind him was Hadley.

Mr. Highborne was so shocked, his hair practically stood on end. (It was a little funny, but a good spy would never laugh under such circumstances.)

"Gaaaah!" he said.

"There you are, Hadley. Mr. Highborne, you remember our friend Hadley. Hadley, you remember Mr. Highborne." I was babbling. Trying not to laugh or throw up. Both were possible.

Hadley gave a shy wave but remained silent.

"Where did you come from?" he demanded, gesturing at our stealthy blond friend.

We all did shoulder shrugs. He just stood there. An icy gleam shone in his eyes.

"Well, as you were saying, I'm sure you have grown-up things to do, and we have, well, kid things to do, so *au revoir*!" I said. We turned, fleeing for the stairs.

"Wait!" he called out, but we quickly raced down the stairs. We didn't stop moving until we were back in the children's parlor. Miss Tutti was still nowhere around.

"Did you get in?" whispered Brooklyn.

Hadley held a tiny memory card between her thumb and finger. She nodded.

"I got in," she said in her small voice. "And I cloned his phone."

Brooklyn reached out her hand, and Hadley placed the chip in her palm. Brooklyn said, "If he checks e-mail from his phone, I'll be able to get into it. We'll see who Mr. Highborne has been talking to."

I said, "And hopefully find out what he's been up to."

CHAPTER 23

The kitchen bustled with activity.

It was the day of the dinner. The entire International PIE Society was present.

In the days since we'd followed Mr. Highborne, nothing surprising had happened. He had not done anything creepier than usual. Brooklyn had downloaded data from his phone, but was having trouble getting into his password-protected files.

Despite all our work, we were no closer to figuring out why he seemed obsessed with the sketchbooks; we didn't know the true identity of Baseball

Cap—and I hadn't seen him since that night with Mama.

I hadn't seen Mama, either.

Waiting was getting so hard.

For once, I was glad for something to distract me from my mission. We were soldiers, and Miss Honey was the colonel of the Pie Brigade.

I was using a big mixer to blend ingredients for the chocolate pie.

"How are you doing, Parlez-Vous?" Brooklyn whispered as we stood together. She leaned into me and said, "Everything's going to be all right. You'll see."

I smiled. "I know," I said, then lowered my voice. "I just can't shake the feeling that I've missed something."

Brooklyn touched my arm, and then, like a shadow, Hadley appeared alongside her.

We followed one of Miss Honey's assistants up the stairs and into the courtyard. Despite the cool autumn nights we'd been having, Papa and his staff had decided to hold the dinner outdoors on long wood-plank tables. A fire pit was being lit. The floor-to-ceiling glass doors separating the courtyard from the inside stood open.

Miss Honey, looking official with her clipboard,

said, "I hope the rain I smell in the air don't get in the way of folks coming to the dinner."

I sniffed. I could also smell the coming rain. The scent of menace was in the air, too.

"Sorry you've been having trouble with your dad," CJ said, sitting down.

I laid my head on top of his and softly said, "Thanks, Zoodle Doodle. We're going to get this all figured out." The whole group gathered around, and in that moment it felt good knowing we had each other's backs.

Pretty soon the room was filling up with people all chatting about museum matters. They arrived at the rear door and entered through the patisserie kitchen, which gave the gathering a warmer, happier feeling.

Albert Cheswick was there, unlit pipe clamped firmly between his teeth. Miss Tutti arrived; so did Magdalena, who ran the museum store, and Leonna, who was in charge of the candy shop attached to the gift shop.

Since I hadn't had much success with the helper

working in the museum store, we figured it couldn't hurt to talk to Magdalena.

"Hey, Maggie, are you ready for the big reopening?" I said after introducing the others.

"Jada, it is so nice to see you!" She grinned, showing a slight gap between her two front teeth. "We're pretty much set for the opening."

After a moment's hesitation, I plunged ahead.

"So, Maggie, Mama shipped a few sketchbooks to me...."

Her eyes widened. "Yes! Just before her...death. You poor girl." She did that tsking thing grown-ups sometimes did. "I was in the shop that day, you know? The day of your mother's accident."

Maggie touched the silver cross hanging around her neck.

"Did you notice anything strange—with Mama, I mean?"

She looked at me curiously. "Strange? With your mom? Well...no. She was her absolutely charming self. I don't want to talk about your mom if this is going to, uh, disturb you."

"No, please," I urged. "I love talking about her. Makes me feel like she's still here."

On the day of her crash, Mama had come into the Sly. Maggie saw Mama casually walking around the museum, enjoying the displays. Mama came into the shop and asked about the sketchbooks. Maggie said her inventory person had accidentally left the prototype designs on the shelf next to the Sly's classic sketchbook.

"Now that I think of it," said Maggie, "I do remember something. I'd been in the middle of telling her about my granddaughter Emmaline, who wants to go to France so bad she can taste it, poor thing, but she's determined to get there....Anyway, I was going on about it when Mrs. Sly's phone rang. She was all business after that."

Maggie didn't know who the caller was, only that Mama went into the corner where the sketchbooks were sitting to finish her call.

"After that," said Maggie, "she hurried up here, paid for your sketchbooks, and was gone. Is there some problem with the sketchbooks? Would rather have the original version than the new one? I know how different the paper is. Some of our artists from the colleges get very fussy about their paper."

She said the last part in a whisper. As if hordes of

angry art students were going to storm the museum store and set the sketchbooks afire.

Big Mike moved forward, his brow furrowed.

He asked, "Miss Maggie, when did the store— the museum—shut down for repairs?"

Her smooth round face looked thoughtful. Finally, she said, "You know, it's funny. We'd been planning the renovation for a while, but a few days after your mother's plane crashed, our plumbing crashed, too!"

"I didn't know that," I said.

"Sweetie, it was a mess around here. Miss Honey, in the kitchen, almost had a conniption," she said.

Hadley asked, "Why? What happened to Miss Honey?"

"Well, she keeps a collection of wigs in her locker, but the locker room was affected, too, and she about had a fit when her wigs were damaged. The kitchen and the museum store got a lot of damage. A week later your father figured it would make more sense to add repairs into the renovation plans," she said.

Looking toward the windows, she added, "It sure is nice of your father to invite us to such an amazing event. I'm so excited for the dinner!"

By the time we left Maggie, we all needed to make sense of what we'd heard. Guests were standing, the faint sounds of classical music floating around them.

The air outside felt thick. It would begin to rain soon, and we'd be forced to come inside.

We carried trays outside. The air had grown warmer. As good as that felt, everyone was crossing their fingers, hoping the rain would stay away.

I spotted Mr. Highborne chatting with a woman from the museum.

My hands tightened into fists. It wasn't fair. He was playing some sort of dangerous game, running around with goons, showing up places he shouldn't be, and I didn't dare say one word to Papa about it.

As if my brain energy lured him to me, Highborne appeared at my side. He had bright blue eyes that pierced into my mind. Was there a law in New York that protected goons from kicks in the shins? Because I really wanted to boot him one good time.

Instead, I kept my feet planted and I glanced back and forth between the other members of our group. I could feel Hadley trying to shrink behind me.

CJ reached out a hand. Mr. Highborne shook it.

"C. J. Effingham the Fourth. My father owns the

Zoodle Doodle company. Maybe you've heard of it,"
he said, smooth as cheese on a cracker. Or…a doodle?

Mr. Highborne looked sideways at CJ. He said,
"Well, of course, bright orange snack puffs are my
life." His tone was dry.

"Allister!" Papa called out from behind us before
we could go any further.

Mr. Highborne glanced at me one more time. It
was as if he was trying to drill some sort of message
into my skull.

He turned toward my father. "Ben!" he said.

Papa led Mr. Highborne away. I remained standing there. Fists knotted.

When I returned to the kitchen to finish helping
with the pies, Hadley followed me. She wore an apol-
ogetic expression, though I had no idea why.

"What is wrong?" I asked.

Granny Grundle, who'd been sitting in a corner
chair, sprang to her feet. The older woman looked
around and said, "The pie smells lovely, dears."

"Thank you, Granny G," Big Mike said.

"Come along, young people," Miss Honey said.
Big Mike and CJ stood taller, puffing out their

imaginary man-sized chests. Hadley, Brooklyn, and I rolled our eyes.

She led us into the patio room. It was time for the guests to be seated.

We took turns assisting Miss Honey, asking who needed water. Once the guests all had plates, it was our turn to find a space and eat.

We were crammed in between grown-ups. I managed to have Brooklyn beside me and Hadley straight across.

I whispered across the table to Hadley. "What happened? You were trying to apologize for something earlier."

It was loud. People were laughing and talking on and on about the great shoe exhibit. Hadley got a gleam in her eyes, and I watched as she slid beneath the table.

I turned to Brooklyn. "She's kidding, right?"

Brooklyn shook her head. "If you want to find out..." She let the sentence hang.

Flicking my gaze side to side, I let out a final sigh, went as limp as possible, and melted beneath the table.

In a forest of pant legs, bare legs, stockinged legs, and plaid legs, Hadley sat glowing, light from her phone filling a small area.

When I managed to escape the forest of legs and toes, we sat across from one another, face-to-face.

Hadley shook her head. She whispered, "By the time Brooklyn and I were able to crack Mr. Highborne's password and look at his e-mail, there was nothing to find."

"Nothing?" I suddenly felt crushed. How was he connected to Mama? Why was he in the car with Baseball Cap?

She shook her head again. Her lips moved, forming the word *nothing*. Then she hesitated.

"One thing," Hadley said. She gave me the one-minute gesture.

"Look!" she said.

I took her phone, careful to avoid the knees of Miss Tutti, who wore lovely flat slippers, by the way. Crawling closer, I peered at the screen.

Hadley whispered, "When I first cloned his phone, this was the only thing I found. One folder. We couldn't open it. Brooklyn has a program that cracks passwords. It finally opened the folder."

With a tap of her finger, she clicked the icon.

The folder was empty.

Hadley and I looked at each other. Disappointment filled her tone. "All that work and breaking into his office for nothing."

She closed the folder and was putting her phone away when I reached out to stop her. I asked to see her phone and stared at the screen.

One folder, with a name typed into a square.

"Umi," I said in a gasp. "It says Umi." I felt light-headed. I touched the screen. Could this be real?

"Sorry we weren't able to find anything helpful. However…" Hadley was talking, but I was sinking underwater. Drowning. I cut her off.

"Hadley, you don't understand. It says 'Umi' on the folder."

She frowned.

"Umi," I repeated. My heart pounded, and my face felt numb. "That's Mama's name."

CHAPTER 24

I had to get out from under the table.

I needed space. I needed fresh air.

Hadley seemed to understand. The light from her phone disappeared, and so did she. I crawled backward but stood so abruptly I slammed my head on the table's underside.

BAM!

First I saw stars as I tried climbing from underneath the table. Then I saw Brooklyn turn quickly in my direction. All I could see was the bountiful halo of her cool 'fro. Behind it, I saw the arched brow and blond hair of Mr. Highborne.

By the time Brooklyn helped me onto my seat, several people at our end of the table had turned in my direction. They all had questioning gazes. A crash of thunder stole everyone's attention.

"Uh-oh, folks," Papa said, grinning. Cécile was at his side. They both beamed with happiness and pride. The party was a success.

Papa said, "We made plans in case this happened."

"No need to break up a good party just because of a little rain," Cécile said. People around the table held up their glasses.

"Cheers!" said the guests.

Another gust of air ruffled the napkins.

Thunder rumbled so close and loud that it rattled the glasses and silverware.

The guests let out a roar of laughter. Then, with Papa leading the way, everyone grabbed their plates and glasses and followed him inside.

"I have to go think," I whispered to Brooklyn.

Miss Honey came over and started telling us kids what we could do to help. I swallowed hard. My mind was so busy I could barely hear her.

Brooklyn looked at me, confused by my behavior. Hadley understood, however.

Hadley whispered in my ear, "Go. Think. We'll cover for you. I'll tell the others what you found."

I didn't know if that was a good idea, telling the others. But I felt too numb to stop her.

Promising to return soon, I slipped away. Papa had allowed me to bring Josephine Baker. Her pen was set up in his office.

Upstairs, I shut the office door and slid onto the floor beside my bunny rabbit.

"Josephine Baker, what am I going to do?" I opened the pen's door, and she hopped out. I ran my fingers along her soft fur. She did several hops at once, kicking her back legs with glee.

I felt...so perplexed. Which means very, very confused!

What in the world was going on? So many clues, and nothing made sense.

Josephine hopped around until she plopped herself onto the fuzzy rug underneath Papa's desk. My sketchbook was stashed there, as well.

I opened it and flipped through the pages.

I found what I was looking for—the new page

of clues, information, and suspicions plaguing my brain.

- Charles and 21 (Where is Charles Tillerson?)
- Who is the man in the baseball cap?
- Mr. Gaston—why track me down like a fugitive and then tattle on me to my dad? Who does that?
- Then there is Mr. Highborne, who has my mother's name in his phone. WHY?!?!?
- Mama

I hadn't written anything else by her name. Too risky. But I sat there thinking about her.

My phone beeped. A text.

It was from Big Mike.

> **WE'RE COMING UP AS SOON AS WE CAN GET AWAY.**

GROWN-UPS ARE DANCING.

SCARY STUFF!!!

I texted that I was in Papa's office.

Then I reached for my pen. I was going to sketch. It always helped me think.

After a little bit, I sat back and stared at my sketches again.

I'd started out trying to remember Charles Tillerson. What he looked like. Anything that would help me find him.

But all I had done was draw poor Mr. Cheswick. I laughed.

Still, for some reason, that made me think of Baseball Cap. Who was he? I hadn't seen him in a while, and I wondered about that, too. Which made me think of the hoodie thief with the long, thin body. Again I remembered how he moved at the airport and again in the subway.

I still hadn't seen the thief's face, but my impression of him kept changing. And why was he going after my art journals?

A sharp rap at the door made me jump. The door opened, and Big Mike stuck his head inside.

"Time to slice the pie," he said. He wore his usual open expression and wide grin. He looked at me and frowned. "What's wrong?"

I had opened my mouth, uncertain what to tell him, when he turned and moved to allow someone else to enter.

"Well, hello!" boomed Albert Cheswick.

His brown pipe twitched between his teeth. He looked around the room. I thought about the sketch I'd done, trying to draw Mr. Tillerson older. It had turned out like Mr. Cheswick. Not exactly, but similar. Ugh! My brain had turned into sad oatmeal.

Now that I looked at him, I could see that the lines didn't match up. Mr. Cheswick's cheeks were rounder, his body softer. Not him. Definitely not.

"What a lovely place you have here, m'love! That beautiful Miss Honey sent me along to fetch you. Now that we've feasted and solved all the world's problems with our wit and intellect, let us eat pie!" he said.

He roared with laughter at his own joke, and

I closed my journal and shoved it back under the desk.

On the way down the stairs, Big Mike put a hand on my shoulder. He whispered, "We found out some information."

We placed slices of pie on small plates in the kitchen, then served the guests. Miss Honey was there with the coffee. Grandmother Sly actually ate her slice of pecan pie.

"Jada, darling," she said. "You and your friends have done an excellent job assisting the staff. And your pies are delicious!"

"Thank you," I said. It was very sweet, but a little embarrassing in front of my friends. "I have to go finish serving."

Time passed; pie was eaten; rain began to patter and blow against the outer doors.

CJ's mother arrived while everyone was talking, laughing, and eating pie. Then I saw CJ looking around.

"Who're you looking for?" I asked.

"My dad," he said. Quickly he added, "But he's very busy making tons of money, so his time is valuable."

I glanced at Papa, suddenly wanting to give him a hug.

When Big Mike's father, the police detective, arrived, my fellow spy raced toward him and almost knocked his father over. Big Mike came back, introduced him, then excused himself to talk to me.

"I want to show you something I found online, but I promised my dad I'd show him around. Can I catch up with you later?"

I said yes and watched him dash away, feeling a familiar prickle on my skin. Something was different—wrong. That was when I looked up the stairway and noticed the window. The front hall stairs wound into the second-floor landing. The window at the end of the hall stood open.

I didn't remember it being opened.

No one was paying close attention to me, so I climbed the stairs. The carpeting and tall ceilings buffered sound. The atmosphere was thick and coarse. Something was going on. I could feel it.

Howling winds and lashing rain began to rage outside. I rushed over and closed the window. Down the skinny hallway, shadows played across the carpet, bringing the ancient patterns to life. I went to the third floor and pushed open the door to Papa's office.

Inside was dark. Quiet.

However, something was different.

Josephine Baker was on top of Papa's desk. She couldn't have gotten there by herself. I swallowed hard.

Much as I'd suspected, beneath the desk was... nothing.

My art journal was gone, *again*!

CHAPTER 25

"Where is it? I know I put it back under the desk," I said to the bunny rabbit. She did not reply.

Looking around the room, I realized the carpet had wet spots. Footprints?

Another crash of thunder rattled the rooftop. The lights flickered on and off. I gasped. My nerves were an utter disaster. When the lights stopped flickering, I commanded myself to pull it together. "All right, Jada Sly, think. What's so special about your art journal?"

The question hung in the silence of the room. I half expected Josephine, whom I'd rescued from the desk and returned to her bedding, to answer. I waited. She remained silent.

The storm was growing more wicked by the minute. People might have to stay the night if this kept up.

As I searched every corner of the office, a thought occurred to me: *What if someone took the art journal because they thought Mama had hidden a valuable piece of evidence inside?*

An honest-to-goodness, high-level piece of intelligence.

I realized that I still had one unused journal hidden inside Papa's grandfather clock in his office. I'd stashed it there after the first one was taken.

I went over to the clock and found the journal. The red leather-bound cover was completely smooth. I gently opened it and ran my fingers over the paper.

One after another, slowly and carefully, I brushed my hand along the thickly layered drawing pages. Until I reached the end of the book. I slid my fingers over the inside of the back cover.

Nothing stood out.

So I did it a second time.

Again, I went all through the book and found nothing. Except...

On the next-to-last page, at the top where the antique coloration created a shadow, I gently dragged my index finger over the area again.

The paper was rough with a raised imprint....

Something was there.

When I stood the journal up, I could see a slight separation between the pressed sheets of paper. I carefully peeled away the bottom half of the sheet. Slowly, a tiny object fell into my hand.

A memory chip. Small as a fingernail.

I picked it up.

Then the lights flickered out.

Darkness filled the room like a living thing.

Until a hot slash of white lightning sent a jagged stripe across the sky.

Lighting the room.

Creating a reflection in the office door.

That was when I saw him.

A shape stepping out of Papa's closet! Tall and rectangular.

And something else. A faint scent. My brain practically exploded. The quick, graceful movements. The scent—light honey and vanilla. Not a shape, but a smell. No wonder I couldn't re-create it in my journal. It was the smell of a girl's body wash. I used it, too.

CHAPTER 26

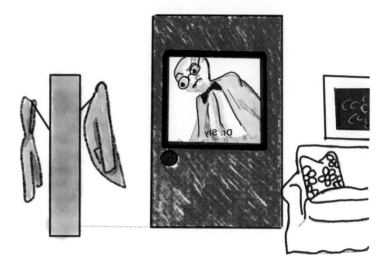

I let out a scream, but quickly a hand reached out and covered my mouth.

"Give me the chip!" said a voice.

I went still. The voice. My stalker wasn't Hoodie Guy. It was Hoodie Girl. I knew it!

She was tall—at least as tall as Papa—and thin. Short waxy blond hair hung past the navy hood, spilling onto my shoulder.

The tiny chip was in my hand. If this creep had broken in here to steal it, it must be important.

"Who are you? What do you want?" I spoke through fingers.

The master at martial arts class taught me one important thing: The art of surprise was about quick thinking. Also, with a bigger, stronger opponent, whatever would free you was okay.

I didn't have time to wonder about anything. I simply reacted.

First, I clamped my teeth onto her finger, and then I bit down with all my might.

She was so shocked that she shoved me.

Before I'd even had time to stumble away, I spun my leg around and connected with the side of her knee. Master Maitre said no bad guy could catch you if he couldn't run.

The young woman—not much older than a teenager—let out a "YOW!" She grabbed her knee as she fell sideways.

Using all my force, I kicked upward, this time connecting with her nose.

I dashed for the door, pausing for only a second. Then I was moving again and didn't stop until I reached the hallway and ran right into Mr. Highborne.

"You!" I said, shouting at his shadowy form.

I backed away. I had known all along he was up to no good.

"Jada," he said, "there are things you don't understand—"

His voice dropped, and he was staring over my shoulder. When I turned, I saw Mr. Albert Cheswick. I ran toward him.

"Jada, no!" shouted Mr. Highborne. Something in his tone slowed me. I turned, and it was like I was in slow motion. Mr. Cheswick. His booming laugh. A laugh that didn't seem to reach his eyes. The rounded chin. The eyes.

Thunder rattled the panes of glass in the hall windows. Jagged-edged lightning sparked against the night sky.

"Mr. Cheswick, Mr. Highborne is trying to hurt me. And there is a girl in my father's office," I said.

Mr. Cheswick pushed open the door and peeked inside.

Then he looked at Mr. Highborne.

"What've you got to say for yourself, Highborne?"

"Cheswick, stay out of this. Jada is in great danger," Mr. Highborne said.

"That is why she is coming with me. Ben sent me

to fetch her. Come along, child," he said, tugging at me. Something made me hesitate. Something in his eyes. Sharp eyes. Round face. Small, poochy lips. Another face popped into my mind. My heart hammered. This couldn't be!

Mr. Highborne lurched toward us.

Sweet old Mr. Albert Cheswick moved as fast as a ninja. He spun and kicked Mr. Highborne so hard I heard the wind whoosh out of him.

Everything was happening so fast.

Mr. Cheswick, wearing a yellow shirt under his suit jacket and with the familiar pipe clamped between his teeth and a walking stick in his hand, turned to me and grabbed my arm with his other hand.

"Playtime is over, you little brat. We know your mother hid the second chip before the crash. I need it now. Be a good girl and give it to your uncle Charlie!" His normally warm, playful gaze had turned hard.

If he hadn't been holding on to my arm so tight, I might've fallen.

"You're Charles Tillerson!" I said.

"In the flesh!"

"You look different than I remember," I said.

Noise from the rain echoed from the roof.

"A little makeup, and a few changes. My British accent had them all fooled. Thank three years in Oxford for that!"

Mr. Highborne still lay limp on the floor.

"Give me the chip, brat, or your father will end up just like your dear old mum!"

Flashes of lightning gave sudden light to the space. Thunder rumbled, making it feel as if the ceiling were pressing down on us. I tried to scramble away from Mr. Tillerson, but he held tight to my arm.

The thief I'd kicked crawled out of the office and pulled herself up. Mr. Tillerson glanced at her.

"You all right, Rebecca?" he asked.

"Watch her, Granddad, the little brat kicks!" she said.

I turned to the man I'd once thought of fondly. "Why did you want to hurt my mother? Why are you betraying your country?"

I was making a guess, but in the spy movies, all the bad guys were betraying their country.

"Shut up!" the fake volunteer said. His once soft, pleasant face was almost purple with rage.

He looked down at me with crazy eyes. He gave me a shake.

"Where is it?" he demanded.

"Let's just get outta here, Granddad," said the six-foot-tall girl in the soaking wet hoodie. "We're running out of time. If she knows where it is, we'll make her talk."

Light filtered down the hall. Faint and thin light, but enough to see the office door start to open. Tillerson noticed, too.

"Who's there? Who's coming out of that room? Show yourself. Or face the consequences," he said.

No one answered.

Then I heard Rebecca yell, "Oh no! Something furry is... YOW! It bit me!"

Josephine Baker to the rescue!

The girl stumbled, and her head knocked against the wall—hard. Then she dropped to the floor with a loud thump!

I took that opportunity to deliver a kick very similar to the one I gave Rebecca to the inside of Mr. Tillerson's knee; however, the older man braced himself.

"Stop it!" he growled.

He didn't let go, but with one last tug I managed to wrench myself free. I stumbled backward, almost falling over Mr. Highborne.

Mr. Tillerson's face grew darker than the stormy sky.

"You little..." He lunged and got hold of my arm again. I yelped.

He wrenched me toward the stairs. To my horror, Granny Grundle was climbing shakily up the steps. Her knitting bag hung from her shoulder.

Mr. Tillerson was so busy tugging me along behind him he didn't see the old woman.

I looked frantically at Granny Grundle. I shook my head.

I thought about all the times I'd imagined myself as a hero. I desperately wanted to do something for Granny G, but she had her head down, determined to get—*somewhere*!

Then she looked at me and placed her finger over her lips.

Mr. Tillerson still had his back to the stairs, dragging me past the freight elevator.

Then a very odd thing happened.

Granny Grundle stood upright.

Mr. Tillerson must have sensed a presence behind him. He whirled around. His grip was so tight I felt like my arm might come off. I was panting and crying a little.

"Well, looky here," Mr. Tillerson said. "Is this

old bag going to come to your rescue, Jada Sly?" His laughter was cold.

He quit laughing when the old lady kicked him in the stomach.

"Granny G!" I said.

Mr. Tillerson went down. Granny did not look afraid at all. Her hair was a little bit crooked, however.

Quite shockingly, Big Mike rolled out of the darkness wielding a mop handle. Mr. Tillerson turned to look at him.

"Ahhh!" Mr. Tillerson said, his voice a high-pitched squeak.

Big Mike's eyes were wide. He said, "That's what I wanted to show you earlier. I just thought it was funny, but now…"

I was panting. "Tell me what?" I said.

"That I finally found another photo of Tillerson and he looked like the old dude volunteering at the museum! Now I know it's because they're the same person," he said.

Down the hallway, Mr. Tillerson's granddaughter was waking up.

I turned to Granny G.

"Are you okay?" I asked. When I laid my hand

on her arm, I could feel her muscles. "Granny, you've got skills," I said.

Brooklyn, CJ, and Hadley appeared beside me.

"Oh no," said Brooklyn. "Parlez-Vous, what's up?"

"He's a bad guy!" I said, pointing. "Mr. Albert Cheswick IS Charles Tillerson. He's been here the whole time. Right under our noses."

While he was still getting to his feet, everyone surrounded him. Granny Grundle, using the deepest voice I'd ever heard, made a command.

"Stay on the ground!" she said. Only, Granny was beginning to sound more like a grandpa.

She swiped at her wig and yanked it off. The glasses, too.

"Are you kids all right?" asked the man.

"Ahh," said Big Mike. "Now the small mustache makes sense."

"It's you!" I pointed at him. The man with the baseball cap.

"Agent Devon Fox, FBI," he said.

Mr. Tillerson stood suddenly and threw a wild punch. His blow connected with Agent Fox, hitting him in the thigh. Then Mr. Tillerson pulled CJ in front of him like a shield.

"I'm getting out of here!" Mr. Tillerson said.

Brooklyn elbow-jabbed him in the neck.

Hadley appeared out of nowhere, hooked her feet between his, and yanked him back to the floor.

He was sputtering. "You lousy kids."

CJ had managed to break free. Agent Fox was reaching toward the traitorous Mr. Tillerson. But this time Mr. Tillerson extended his walking stick. He clicked a button, and a needle popped out.

Was it filled with poison?

"Kids, look out!" said Agent Fox.

Mr. Tillerson tried to turn toward the agent, but he wasn't fast enough. Fox dove toward him, tackling him and batting away the walking stick, which flew straight through the glass in Papa's office door. Hadley fell sideways.

Agent Fox held down Mr. Tillerson. Out of nowhere, Rebecca was up, trying to pull Agent Fox off her criminal partner.

"We have to do something!" I said to the others.

Big Mike, who was now behind the thief, hit her on the head with the mop handle. Rebecca, who clearly had some martial arts skills, executed a move that our teacher hadn't taught us yet.

Big Mike took a second swipe, grabbing the mop handle and tossing it down the hall, but then Rebecca kicked Big Mike, sending him flying against the wall.

He crashed hard, making an *oomph* sound.

Agent Fox was still getting the best of Mr. Tillerson. Until Rebecca attacked.

Hadley, Brooklyn, and I jumped in to help, but as soon as Fox began grappling with Rebecca, Mr. Tillerson threw Hadley and Brooklyn to the floor.

"Last chance," he said, grabbing me, blood dripping from his nose. "Tell me where it is, you lousy brat, or I'll strangle you and your friends!"

The pocket where I'd stashed the chip rode upward from the force of him pulling on me.

Not thinking, I automatically reached down to secure it.

"You have it on you?" he asked. His tone was deadly.

I didn't even have time to answer. He tore into my pockets, snatched out the chip, and shoved me to the floor with such effort I bounced.

He and his limping granddaughter took off for the stairs leading to the roof.

"Jada! Are you okay?" Hadley and Brooklyn knelt beside me. Agent Fox, who appeared to be in a broken heap at the foot of the stairs thanks to Rebecca shoving him, was shaking his head, trying to clear it.

"We can't let him get away," I said. My throat was hoarse from yelling, crying, fighting.

CJ was holding his phone. "Help is on the way," he said. "I'm going to go downstairs and get the grown-ups!"

Agent Fox tried to talk. "No…" he was saying.

"CJ, wait," I said. "I don't think he wants you to get the other grown-ups."

The knitting bag Agent Fox had been carrying as part of his disguise lay on the floor behind him. When he pointed to it, I picked it up and took it to him.

He rummaged inside the big granny bag without looking. When he removed his hand, he was holding a small black phone.

"It's Fox," he said into it. "We need a team here now! Tillerson made a play for the girl. He has the chip. We can't let him escape, but he went—" He looked at me.

"To the roof, I think," I said, in answer to his question. Agent Fox groaned.

He said into the phone, "He's trying to escape from the roof. That means he must have a helicopter coming."

The person on the other end said a bad word, and Agent Fox looked up, knowing I could hear. Then he told the person, "I think my leg is broken. I can't stand up."

I ran back up and checked on Mr. Highborne. His eyes opened and he groaned. "I'm fine, kid. But someone has to stop them. Can't…" He grimaced and I tried not to freak out.

"Hadley, could you get some ice for Mr. Highborne? And we really need an ambulance!" I said.

CJ leaned over him, too, taking his pulse. He started telling me some story about his father, but I wasn't listening.

At our last PIE Society meeting, we'd discussed using whatever you had available to protect yourself. An idea occurred to me, and I ran.

The second-story pantry was where the kitchen staff stored some cooking items.

Inside I pulled a string attached to a light bulb. A faint glow filled the space. Quickly, I grabbed what I needed.

"Jada!" called Brooklyn.

"Here I come!" I answered.

She was standing at the top of the stairs. Concern touched every angle of her face.

"I'm going to call the police, Jada. I'll let the grown-ups know," Brooklyn said.

"No!" I said. "Agent Fox has called for backup. He doesn't want the grown-ups from the party up here in case anything else happens. We need to go downstairs and wait for the FBI, and try not to let anyone else up the stairs."

She stared curiously at me. "Are you coming?" she asked.

"In a minute," I said, trying to conceal the items in the bag I was carrying.

She wasn't fooled.

"Be careful!" she said.

Brooklyn rounded up the others and relayed the message. As soon as they were heading downstairs, I moved slowly in the opposite direction.

I crept up the narrow access stairs and pushed at the hatch. It barely budged. The wind and rain were making it harder to open the door.

After taking a deep breath, I used all the ballet strength I had and shoved myself up and through, into the darkness and danger that awaited.

CHAPTER 27

Rain lashed.

The wind roared.

In the distance, lights flickered. Not lightning.

They were lights on an airplane. Or a helicopter.

The weather forced the gray shadow to sway like a ship on a rocky ocean. I crouched. Mr. Tillerson and his limping relative were hunkered down across the rooftop.

How on earth was I going to get that chip away from them?

I stood, trying to ease around the skylights that

stuck out like metal flags to deflect water away. They were also excellent for providing cover on the rooftop.

My chances weren't good, but I had to try. I was about to step out of the shadows to stop the two traitors when I heard a voice say softly, "No, *baby*, no!"

"Mama?"

Arms wrapped around me. Tight and fierce. Thunder rattled the window frames that looked out from the attic space.

Mama quickly ended the hug. There was business to attend to.

She tapped her lips with two fingers.

Quiet.

She placed her lips close to my ear. "Do they have the chip?" she said.

I nodded.

She pointed, indicating that I needed to stay hidden. I shook my head.

"I'm coming with you, Mama. You need me," I said.

Mr. Tillerson was peering through the darkness in our direction.

"Who's over there?" he yelled.

We looked at each other—my mother and I—and we knew time was not on our side.

"It's now or never, kiddo. Show me what you've got!" she said. Then she told me exactly what she needed me to do.

She stepped out of hiding, moving from behind the smokestack.

"Charles, how could you?"

"Well, well, well," said Mr. Tillerson. "If it isn't everybody's favorite dead spy. Why couldn't you just leave well enough alone? You had to keep digging. You weren't satisfied until you'd identified all twenty-one agents who were accepting money from the Chinese. Including me!"

Another flash of lightning. The dark sky was taking on a sickly shade of green. The wind seemed to be blowing in all directions at once.

Mama made her move, dropping into a fighting stance. "Give up before I make you give up!"

Now, picture this:

Mama with her rain-soaked hair plastered against her cheek, her trench coat whipping in the breeze. Facing two international criminals who've proven they aren't afraid to terrorize children.

Mr. Tillerson and his villainous granddaughter inching closer to Mama. She seemed so alone out there.

The helicopter hovering above, its lights swaying wildly.

And me? I was ready for battle. I took my first weapon from the plastic bag I'd brought with me.

Cooking oil.

While the Tillersons approached Mama, I circled around them. When they couldn't see me, I poured oil on the wet rooftop. Then I got out of the way.

That was when they charged!

Mama's kicks were awesome. Little Miss Tillerson, on the other hand, stumbled backward. Her shoe hit the oil-slickened roof. She skidded, arms windmilling.

Then *crash*!

She had tripped over her own feet and slammed into a fan grate. Rain and wind plastered her corn-colored hair against her skull. She was lucky the turbine fan was covered with a sturdy metal cage.

Still, when she tried standing again, she had trouble balancing herself.

Meanwhile, Mama needed my help.

Mr. Tillerson lunged at her again. His blow caught

her on the shoulder. Time for my second weapon. Two rolling pins.

Mama was able to push him back just enough. I bent low and swung the first rolling pin into his ankle. Right on the ankle bone. He screamed. I placed the other rolling pin under his foot. When he stepped down, he fell like a cartoon villain.

"Your daughter is as crazy as you are!" he said. He was yelling. Mama was circling. I was doing whatever I could to protect my mother. And maybe the free world!

"Give up, Charles!" Mama said. "Besides, Rebecca hardly seems stable herself. What have you done to her, Charles? She used to be such a sweet little girl. Now you've turned her into—what?"

"A survivor!" he said with a snarl.

He'd made it to a ledge and was pulling himself up with great effort.

"You shouldn't have been such a goody-goody," he said. I understood what he was trying to do—give the helicopter pilot enough time to get into position.

"You were putting good agents at risk. You and twenty of your pals," Mama said.

"You should've stayed dead," Mr. Tillerson purred.

"When this is all over, I'll have to kill you—AGAIN! Now excuse me, I have a flight to catch."

He reached for a ladder the helicopter pilot had dropped down. Where'd he find some guy willing to fly a helicopter in this weather? Criminal Airways?

I could see Mama was thinking what I was thinking: *Don't let him on that helicopter.*

We both charged after him, causing him to leap for the ladder.

Limber as he was, Mr. Tillerson wasn't a young man. Catching a wiggly chain ladder dangling from a helicopter during a thunderstorm might be easy for a Navy Seal, but it wasn't so easy for an older gentleman.

The ladder dangled beside him, but as he reached for it, Mama kicked at him from behind.

When he spun around, rage filled his expression. Wet fringes of white hair clung to his head. Red lights beneath the helicopter reflected off his bald spot.

"Won't you give up?" he growled, punching at Mama.

The blow struck her on the shoulder. She stumbled. The ladder hung right above his head now.

Think! Think! Think!

Cooking oil had been enough to stop his granddaughter, but for this moment I needed something bigger.

I stepped back several feet. Mama lay on the roof, trying to get up, stunned from the awful blow to her body.

While ballet had always been my preferred method of exercise, I spent quite a bit of time learning gymnastics, too. Those girls knew all about power.

I took off at a run. My heart was zinging away. This wasn't an action scene I was making up in my head. And it wasn't something I was doing to keep from coping with something else.

Right now, in this moment, what I was doing was taking action. If I didn't help stop this man, real lives would be in danger.

Especially Mama's!

Front handsprings. The momentum gives you great power.

That was what I needed.

I went into front handsprings.

One, two, three...

Fast as I could.

When I got to the final one, there was just enough

time to catch the puzzled expression on Mr. Tillerson's face as he glimpsed me at first, then turned, puzzled as to what I was doing. His hand was grasping at the ladder.

Then...

With the final flip, I went into rotation to get more height, then—CRACK!—kicked him right in the face. So it was a gymnastics and tae kwon do combo.

Mr. Tillerson staggered. By now Mama was back on her feet. She went over and punched him in the face.

Jittery lights on the bottom of the helicopter rose higher and higher into the night sky. Mr. Charles Tillerson lay in a crumpled heap of wet clothing.

Mama wasted no time. She knelt over him, patting his pockets. It didn't take long to find what she was looking for.

"I was in such a panic when I was at the Sly that day that I accidentally sent you the journal I was supposed to be hiding in the museum. But I didn't know that. Allister took a job here as a cover so he could take his time and retrieve it," she said.

"Did Allister cause the trouble with the gift shop plumbing?" I asked, remembering what Miss Maggie had said.

Mama smiled. "You are smart," she said. "Allister did that, but he wasn't anticipating that Ben would order a full renovation. Before Allister could even get settled, Ben had all the inventory moved and the whole place was in full-blown disaster mode. Meanwhile, I've been hiding out in places all over the globe, trying to get more intel and maintain the fiction of my death."

At that moment, the access door flew open. Swarms of people wearing navy windbreakers with FBI lettering ran onto the roof. Mama shrank into the shadows.

"They can't know about me," she said.

"Mama, they're—"

"I know who they are."

Above, the helicopter that had come for the Tillersons turned in the night sky, ready to retreat, only to be stopped by two FBI helicopters hanging like black raptors. They were going to make the pilot land.

It was all over.

I turned to look back at Mama.

But she was already gone.

CHAPTER 28

Mama was alive.

But she was also gone.

The day after the museum dinner, the sun was a bright ball in the morning sky. Thanks to a call from Grandmother Sly, Mrs. Vicario had allowed me to take a break from class. I'd stepped out into the garden. In the dense thicket of trees bordering the school property stood Mama.

We'd been sitting on an iron bench, feeling each other's warmth seep through our clothing. Our time was ticking away.

"Are you sure you have to go?" I asked for the hundredth time.

"It's for the best," she said, her eyes sad but her manner resolute. "Gavin—Mr. Gaston, as you know him—was second in command back then. He suspected Charles but didn't have any proof. However, when I turned in the original data chip, Charles immediately destroyed it, instead of authenticating it as he should have. I couldn't believe it."

"How did you find out?" I said.

"Gavin called me. I was in the museum gift shop at the time. He said I couldn't trust Charles, and I shouldn't get on the plane."

Mama said she'd come up with a plan to hide a copy of the chip inside the museum, suspecting she'd get mugged—or worse—the moment she left. She was going to return and get the hidden sketchbook later.

"I was robbed," she said. "They ran off with a sketchbook. The one I'd bought for you. Only it wasn't the one with the chip."

She sighed and led me away from the school property. We crossed the street and walked in silence along the sidewalk beside Central Park for a while. I was sore, tired, and shaken from the night before.

"What about Allister Highborne?" I said.

She gave a short little laugh. "I told Allister not to underestimate you," she said with a shake of her head. "We were partners. But Gavin couldn't bring him in on our ruse, not right away. Once we learned we'd have to get the backup copy of the microchip, Allister managed to get hired at the museum."

"I can't believe you work with that guy," I said, still unwilling to give Mr. Highborne any credit.

"Baby, he always had your best interest at heart. Believe me!"

We found a bench wedged into a nook and sat.

"Mama, if you and Mr. Highborne both knew Charles Tillerson, why didn't Mr. Highborne recognize Cheswick for who he was?"

She was holding a small cup of coffee. She took a sip. "Simple. Charles always was a master of disguise. After all, he disguised himself as a patriot for years."

After the crash, Mr. Gaston had helped her stay in hiding.

"Searching the museum, however, turned out to be a daunting task. Every time Allister thought he'd looked everywhere, he'd come across another storage closet full of boxes filled with more gift shop inventory."

She took another sip from her coffee.

"Charles had left the company," she said.

"You mean the Caspian Group?"

She smiled. "No, Caspian was a cover. The entire office was full of agents."

"CIA?" I asked.

She shook her head. "We were a special elite group that did all kinds of operations all over the world. And we did publish books, too," she said.

"Did you know about Agent Fox watching me and going undercover as a chaperone at our school?" I still couldn't shake the picture in my head of Agent Fox in that dress. He made such a sweet old lady. I was going to miss Granny Grundle.

Mama said she'd known the Yankees-loving Agent Fox since they were at Columbia together. Even then, she said, he wore baseball caps all the time. She'd had Highborne make contact with him. They tipped the FBI agent off about an operation Charles Tillerson was planning with some foreign agents.

"Fox was our eyes and ears inside. Allister also told him that you might be in danger. He was protecting you, he said, because he hadn't been able to protect me."

Mama said Charles Tillerson had gone insane with worry and anger when he learned someone was planted inside the Sly to retrieve the missing computer chip.

He'd sent a few agents inside himself but never got anywhere. Finally, desperate to conceal the information that would send him to prison, he'd posed as a volunteer so he could look, too. And enlisted aid from his own granddaughter—a failed agent too klutzy to pass the physical to get into the CIA.

"And Mr. Highborne isn't really a creep?"

"You've got skills, kid—I'll give you that," said a voice. Allister Highborne stepped into view. He looked at Mama.

"Umi," he said, "we have to go."

We'd been hanging on to each other, but I knew she would have to leave.

I didn't want her to.

"What about Papa and Cécile?" I said. Even I knew the answer, but I wasn't ready to let go.

"Be happy for Papa. I am. Right now, it is still important for me to remain hidden. Tillerson will be put into a hole so deep he won't be able to blab to anyone. There were twenty other names on that chip with details of their crimes. They all must pay."

In a small voice, I said, "But you and Daddy are still married."

She looked at me with sad eyes.

"Only if I come back to life," she said.

She pulled me tight again and said, "Take it easy on your dad. Benjamin and I, well, he's a good guy. A good man. He deserves some happiness." Then she whispered, "You never saw me, Jada Marie."

"How could I? You died in a plane crash."

"But my heart will always be alive, as long as you're in it," she said.

"Umi," Mr. Highborne said quietly.

She nodded.

Before she disappeared completely, she said urgently, "No matter what, Jada Marie Sly. Remember that I love you."

"Will I see you again?"

"Count on it."

And just like that, my first spy mission was over. My heart ached, but now that Mama was alive, I knew I'd be okay.

Especially as long as I had my PIE Society posse. They had my back. And I had theirs.

Right now, that was all I needed.

EPILOGUE

Papa was beaming when I saw him at the museum after school. The dinner party had been a success, despite the international criminal waging war on his roof. No way he knew anything about what happened. Or about Mama.

Soon after the FBI arrived that night, Homeland Security showed up. So did a bunch of other agencies.

They told Papa that there was an imminent threat in the area. By the time they evacuated the museum, mostly everyone was gone, anyway. Papa took Cécile and me home.

When our doorbell rang later that evening, Papa was on the phone joyfully recounting some bit of museum news. The change in his tone when he opened the door caused me to pause.

A few seconds later, he called, "Jada! Could you come down for a minute, please?"

I gave Josephine Baker a pat and slid off the bed. When I reached the foyer, I was shocked at what I saw.

Standing in front of Papa was Mr. Gaston.

"Hello, Miss Sly," said the man in his soft voice.

I did a small wave. Papa looked between us.

With a slight smile, Mr. Gaston said, "I wanted to check on you and make sure you're okay."

"I'm okay."

I turned to Papa. Mr. Gaston did, as well. "Benjamin, do you mind if I speak with your daughter? I'll only be a minute."

Papa asked, "Jada?"

"It's okay, Papa. I'll be fine."

We went into the library. The windows looked onto the side of the next house.

"Well, Miss Sly, it's good to see you again," he said.

We both stood with our backs to the room, staring out the floor-to-ceiling windows.

In his low, calm way, he said, "I'm glad things worked out. I hear you were a big part of our success. Thank you."

I tried to hold back my smile. I nodded. "I was only trying to help." A moment passed. Then I said, "And thank you."

He stared down at me. "For what?"

"Helping Mama," I said. "She told me what you've done for her. I'm glad you're on her side."

He turned back, facing the window. He gave a small nod and said, "It is very important that her cover story remain intact. If anyone finds out she's alive, it could compromise not only her safety, but yours and your father's, as well."

"I understand," I said.

"Good," he said softly. When I looked at him, he wore the barest of smiles.

"Miss Sly, it was good working with you. Perhaps we can do it again sometime," he said.

I felt a familiar frisson.

"For real?" I asked.

"You never know. If the right case came along, well…"

He reached out and took my hand. I shook his.

Then he said good-bye and was gone.

On Sunday, Papa took Cécile, Grandmother Sly, me, and Brooklyn out to dinner.

We were eating pasta again because spaghetti and meatballs are my absolute favorite. Everyone was laughing and talking. It was a good night.

Up ahead, I noticed a large, boxy truck. It careened a bit. I thought about the night I'd been convinced I saw a truck filled with criminals. This time I shook away the image.

Brooklyn leaned over and whispered, "Jada, I'm sorry about your mom. I know you were hoping to find her alive. But you were right about the man following you."

That was the official story.

Allister Highborne left the museum to pursue another case. The PIE Society, however, was convinced he'd been fired and shipped to some unknown prison along with his friend Charles Tillerson.

Brooklyn said, "I read in a brochure that your

father is bringing artifacts from Egypt to do a mummy exhibit. There has to be some sort of mystery involved with that for us to investigate."

"You never know," I said, doing my best impersonation of Mr. Gaston. One thing was for certain:

More mysteries lay ahead. I had no doubt!

ACKNOWLEDGMENTS

I need to acknowledge my editor, Ms. Nikki Garcia, for supporting this idea from the beginning. Nikki, you shepherded this project when at some points I know you must have questioned my sanity or perhaps your own. Thank you for believing that Jada's story was not only worth telling, but also worth seeing. I would also like to acknowledge my agent, Laurie Liss at Sterling Lord Literistic. Thank you for accepting all my visions and for giving me an opportunity to bring out all my creative sides.

And a special acknowledgment to all the illustrators I've met over the past ten years of dreaming of the day this book would be a reality. Artists who, when cornered at conferences, graciously offered encouragement and even tips. I am humbled by all your thoughtfulness.

Thank you to all who saw enough in me to tell me to keep going. I am so proud to finally bring this story to life.

Turn the page for a preview of

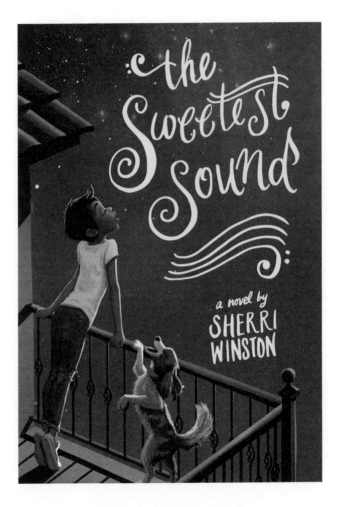

AVAILABLE NOW

Prelude

Birthdays are a problem for me. It's been that way for almost four years. My seventh birthday was the last time life felt normal. My party was amazing. We ate dinner at a Mexican restaurant, just family and a few friends—the way I like it. One of my friends, Faith, is from the Dominican Republic, so even though people assume she's African American, she speaks Spanish quite well, thank you very much! She taught us some words. The band played "Happy Birthday to You!" the Spanish way, and we sang *"Feliz cumpleaños a ti."* The music felt like sunshine on my skin, and Faith, Zara, and I did silly dances. My mother even sang with the band.

It was the best night. Just the absolute best!

The next morning I found a note on the coffeepot. It read:

> *I love you all so much. But I have to pursue my passion. I can't grow in Harmony, can't be a star here. Jeremiah, you are a great man, wonderful husband, and terrific father. Cadence and Junior are lucky to have you. You deserve to be loved more than I can offer. Please don't hate me. Cadence, my sweet little Mouse, so quiet and shy. Always remember, you are the high note of my life. I will always love you.*
>
> *Chantel Marie Jolly*

And then, she was gone.

Birthdays have been tricky ever since.

My name is Cadence Mariah Jolly.

I live in western Pennsylvania in a small town called Harmony.

I'm up in the middle of the night because I simply cannot sleep. Last year I stood outside my bedroom on this very balcony, staring past the dark mountaintops, pleading for a miracle. If God answered my prayers it would be a sign. No more sad, weird birthdays.

That's what I thought. Truly.

Funny thing, though. God answered my prayers. I got exactly what I wanted.

Now, four weeks away from my next birthday, that blessing feels more like a curse.

I read a book over the summer called *Holes*. It was about this kid, Stanley Yelnats, who got sent away to an awful juvie place in the desert for something he didn't even do. Talk about a curse! It was a great book, and I've reread it a few times. I plan to be a No. 1 Bestselling Author of Amazing Stories one day, so I like to study the works of other authors.

I love reading, because authors have an amazing gift— they see problems and they find solutions. Have you ever wondered how an author would fix your life in a book? If the author of *Holes*, Louis Sachar, wrote a book about me, would he write about the fact that I'm really quiet? That at times I like being alone? Would he write about how I get this shaky, dry-mouthed feeling that makes my heart race whenever I'm around a lot of people? And if he did write a story about a girl like me, one who loves to read and plans to write great stories, a girl who is quiet yet tired of getting talked over and overlooked, tired of being pitied, how would Mr. Sachar fix her? (Me?)

Trust me. I've got lots that need fixing.

All I asked God for was one thing: for Daddy to find a way to get me a Takahashi 3000x keyboard and microphone. (It's the kind used by all the best Internet sensations! At least, that's what Faith says.)

In my prayers, I promised I'd share my secret talent with the world, if only God made my dream come true. My aunt and lots of people at church were always warning us kids about our prayers. *God ain't no Santa Claus,* they liked to say. *When you talk to the Lord, be mindful of what you're asking for. A prayer is a powerful thing.*

Honest, I believe in God, but truthfully, I wasn't quite convinced He'd even care about my keyboard or my secret.

Until it happened. God granted my wish. It was like some kind of miracle.

Somehow Daddy got his hands on a busted-up Takahashi 3000x and fixed it without me finding out. Next thing you know, I get the keyboard for my birthday. A real dream come true.

Now it's time to keep my promise. But I don't think I can.

What happens if you make a promise to God, then try to take it back?

1

Underneath the Stars

Some words feel so grown-up when you say them. Like *scintillating*. I whispered the word like it was part of a magic spell. One of many astronomy terms I learned from my mother. It means twinkling like stars. When she taught it to me, she would say it, then tell me to repeat it, and touch my lips as I did. Said to let it tumble from my mouth.

My mother loved staring into the night sky. She loved pointing out groups of stars called constellations. She told me *I* loved it, too. Which was funny, because I could have sworn that staring into the sky at distant planets and glowing dust used to scare me. It made me feel so small, like I was vanishing. All I knew about the sky and the stars was what my big brother, Junior, had told me. Which was that slimy aliens and space monsters lived out there—he knew it because someone named Captain Kirk told him so. Like I knew the difference between Captain Kirk and Cap'n Crunch.

I told her once, my mother, that looking into the deep vastness of the sky made me afraid. She surprised me, saying it used to do the same to her. She said she'd wondered as a kid about the universe with all of its mysteries, but she figured its mysteriousness was part of its beauty.

She was so convinced that I loved it as much as she did that she ordered a telescope as a gift for my fifth birthday.

Don't get me wrong. I did get quite a few things that I loved, too. Such as a tiny iPod and multiple pairs of candy-colored earbuds. I love music. My favorite singer was (and still is) Mariah Carey. She is like my fairy godmother. If fairy godmothers were real, which they aren't. Except...maybe. I haven't quite figured that out. Anyway, I had listened to my Mariah playlist for so long, it was as if her songs were made to explain all the chapters of my life.

Later on, of course, my mother was gone, but the night sky no longer freaked me out. I gazed into the tiny lens of the telescope because seeing the stars up close made me feel closer to her. I knew that Captain Kirk was a make-believe character in *Star Trek*, and aliens and space monsters were make-believe, too. Probably.

I also knew that most of the time, especially lately, I was the one who felt like an alien. Staring into the heavens, I imagined stories about the planets and the moon. Outer space didn't make me feel invisible anymore; people did.

Darkness wrapped around me. I pressed my eyes shut and remembered the touch of my mother's fingertips on my skin.

When I opened my eyes, her image appeared in the sparkling mass of constellations. The shape of her face was Cassiopeia; her eyes, Polaris; the curve of her neck, the handle on the Big Dipper. Just the way I remembered her, before she left us. Beautiful and distant. *Scintillating.*

I used to get lost in the shadow of her shine. She was so beautiful and talented that it was like she cast this bright glow, you know? And the light from her amazingness reached way up into the heavens. I could never, ever come close.

When she left, our world slipped into darkness. Would it be that way forever?

♪♫ ♪

Our house is three stories high. The top floor is like my apartment—I have it all to myself since my mother left and Daddy said he couldn't face being up here alone. He and Junior carted all my things up from the first floor because Junior said he didn't want to be up here, either.

Now it's just me and the last wonderful gift my mother ever gave me: my floppy-eared spaniel terrier, Lyra. She'd say hi, except it's late. Really late. And Lyra loves her beauty sleep.

Holding Lyra close, I leaned back on the chair and took in the night sky. My imagination conjured a familiar story. One that absolutely, positively made me sway. The way you might if you stood up too fast and got light-headed.

The story came out of my soul, and now it rests in a journal. All good writers keep journals. When I grow up, I will write wonderful stories about girls who are brave and wise and fearless. Girls unafraid to stand out. Girls nothing like me.

So, in the story I made up, my mother is no longer absent. She's returned. She is in awe of my writing talent. She loves me so much and wishes she had not left me back when I was a little kid.

We are being interviewed on TV. The host has tears in her eyes talking about my amazing new book. She says with a name like Cadence Mariah, it's no wonder my words flow like a song, no wonder I grew up playing the piano and singing in my school and church choirs. The TV host understands. *Cadence* means "rhythm." Middle name, Mariah, as in the famous singer, Mariah Carey. (See why I feel like she's my fairy godmother?)

Now, in my story, which flashes across the purplish mountainside like in a movie on a theater screen, I see the whole scene so clearly. I'm laughing with the interviewer, a quiet little laugh, and explaining how I used to be so shy that I hid in the back rows of the choirs.

My mother, I reveal to the talk show lady, is known throughout our hometown for sounding like the famous singer Whitney Houston. When I was born, Daddy says, she couldn't bear to share the perfection of Miss Houston with me. Instead, she made my middle name the same as her second-favorite singer, Miss Mariah Carey. But to me, Miss Mariah would always be No. 1!

The TV show lady, tears glittering in her eyes, begs the two of us to sing a song together.

My mother says, *No, she couldn't.* She says, *My baby won't sing because she is so shy.*

And then the TV show lady looks at me. Eyes pleading.

I walk over to my mother. I am very confident and sophisticated. The youngest bestselling author in the whole, entire world. She does not know how much I've changed since she left us. I am different now. Not the same Mouse.

I say, *Okay, Mother. I will sing with you.* In a totally low-voiced, dramatic sort of way.

And then we stand in the middle of the stage. My mother slips her hand into mine. Then the music begins.

The orchestra knows exactly what song to play. The only song that makes sense:

"When You Believe."

It is the only duet between the great Miss Houston and the amazing Miss Mariah.

When we begin to sing, my mother stares in disbelief. She cannot believe how beautiful my voice is. She always wanted me to be a singer. Like her. But I don't think she believed it would happen. I was always too shy. Was that why she left us?

She did try to be happy as a wife and mother, working part-time at the Superstar Gas n' Grocery Mart while taking classes at the community college.

But that kind of life was making her die inside, Daddy said. He said somebody like my mother was born for bigger things. He said we did not wish her ill, but would, in fact, pray for her success and joy and happiness. Like my mother, Daddy seemed to think he knew what I was feeling without even asking. And even though my mother sent me a phone as a gift, she rarely called or left a number where I could reach her. Still, I told myself that was okay. I would hold no grudges; I told myself I forgave her. In my heart, I hoped it was true.

So, in my story, my incredible, amazing, can't-put-down, make-believe story, there we are. Reunited.

And singing.

It is the best feeling in the whole wide world.

I stared into the sky.

The stars were twinkling their applause. My heart danced in its cage. Lyra snuggled up to my ankles and let out a low doggie moan. I reached down and scruffed her neck. She was a small white dog with spots of golden and chocolate brown spattered over her face and ears. I named her after the constellation Lyra, which was itself named for an instrument played in Greek mythology.

While my mother believed in all kinds of mythology, Daddy was a man who believed in keeping his feet firmly on the ground. When he wasn't busy working for the sheriff's department as a deputy or helping with the high school football team as an assistant coach, his real love was fixing old instruments. He actually had an instrument in his shop called a lyre. It made the coolest sounds. He had something else called a lute. Sort of like an old-fashioned guitar with a potbelly. I loved the lute and begged him to teach me how to play it, so he did. He refinished one and gave it to me as a gift.

My fingers trailed across the strings of the lute now resting on my lap. A weird hollow feeling deep inside my chest made me shake inside out.

Slumping beneath the quilt thrown across my shoulders, I sank into the creaky wooden chair. Lyra stirred, then she hopped onto my lap, pushing the lute aside. The warmth of her body, the scent of her doggie shampoo, made me draw a deep, calming breath. My fingers casually strummed the belly of the handmade instrument, the notes sad and sweet like tree boughs singing in the wind.

I like to think that my mother gave me Lyra because she wanted someone here to watch over me—all of us— while she went out into the world to make her dreams come true. She was a singer, and a singer needed to sing.

So I wished her the very best. Tried to, anyway.

I breathed in air that was cold and tasted like winter, even though the calendar still said fall. It felt so peaceful. I inhaled the quiet back into my lungs.

Then the peacefulness gave way to a knocking beat in my chest. My heart skipped a scratchy, snare drum rhythm. The lute's music sounded melancholy. Another excellent grown-up word—*melancholy*. I was having trouble concentrating. Partly because of the secret I was hiding. And partly because of the promise I had yet to keep.

Last year, sitting right here, I prayed and prayed for Daddy to find a way to buy me the keyboard. And I promised God I'd stop being so boring and scared and start taking chances. No. 1 Bestselling Authors of Amazing Stories get their ideas from being bold, not by hiding from EVERYTHING.

I was too shy and too scared. I did have to hand it to my mother about one thing, though—piano lessons. I started playing at three years old, and even though I still get butterflies sometimes, I know I'm pretty good.

The music teacher at school and choir director at church knew about our family. Everyone did. Funny thing having a whole town pity you. Everyone bending over backwards to "help." They tolerated my shyness. I hid behind other singers so I wouldn't throw up on anybody's shoe. But when the music teachers or directors needed me, I could play the piano or keyboard well enough to help. It worked out well for everybody.

Replacing my dinky little keyboard with a Takahashi 3000x got me singing around the house all the time. Well, when I was alone, that is. I loved how singing touched my heart and made me feel light. Powerful. Strong. I wished I had the courage to sing in front of real people.

Once I realized how good it felt, singing out loud with all my heart, mumble-singing in the back rows of the choir became more difficult. Still, I was determined not to draw attention to myself. I got enough attention for being the girl whose mother left. Everybody treated me like I was made of glass. Like I was broken.

Am I broken? Would I know it if I were?

One day Reverend Shepherd had given a sermon about

blessings. He said God has anointed each of us with special gifts and talents. He said ignoring them was a sin. He said we should stand in our blessings, which I'd figured meant if God gave you a talent, you were supposed to use it. Kind of like a superpower.

You know, church is like that. Sometimes the pastor is talking and all you can think about is eating pancakes when he is done. But sometimes he says something and, just like that, it feels like he's talking absolutely, positively to YOU. I got chills as he talked about keeping our talents a secret.

"God knows all your secrets," he'd said. I practically ducked down in my seat.

Honestly! Fear and guilt followed me like a cloud. I'd promised to use my voice to sing loud and stop being shy if He granted my wish. But I wasn't sure I was ready to do that.

Maybe I needed some kind of sign. Like when Moses struck the rock and it flowed with water in Numbers 20:10–11. Or in Matthew 14:17–21 when He fed the multitudes with loaves and fishes. I mean, in Bible School, we learned that when God gives us a sign, we need to pay attention. We understood that if you have faith, God will deliver miracles.

While I waited for a sign, I kept practicing at my piano teacher's house. Mrs. Reddit was also the music teacher at my school; she gave lessons on the side. One day while we were practicing, she had gone to make a call, and I got caught up in one of the pieces—"His Eye Is on the Sparrow"—and began to sing. The words did not get caught in my throat or stumble over my lips. They passed through my heart, one by one, until they rose up to the chandelier above the dining room table. Singing with all my soul made me feel free and beautiful and loved.

Until I finished and realized Mrs. Reddit was standing right there.

Then I felt trapped and terrified and exposed.

My heart started pounding. My face felt hot and itchy. But part of me truly also wondered if she thought I was as good as I'd begun to think I was—even though I didn't want to think about being good at all.

And sure enough, she said, "Cadence, was that really you? That was the most amazing thing, child. How long have you been singing like that?"

She saw the terror in my eyes. Saw me start to shake. She rushed over. Wrapped her long, thin arms around me. Hugged my body into her powdery perfume softness.

"Please don't tell. Please don't tell. Please don't tell," I whispered over and over again. I wasn't even sure who I thought she'd tell. I just knew I didn't want anyone else finding out.

Mrs. Reddit, being so awesome and all, promised it would be our secret. "When you're ready to sing in public, you will. I hope one day you will trust me with your gift and let me show you how to make it shine," she said.

After that, even when I was hiding in the back row of choir in her class, Mrs. Reddit never mentioned my singing again.

But now, my two best friends, Zara and Faith, were counting on me. In a little less than a month, I'd be turning eleven. An important age in choir years. At church, eleven was how old you had to be to go from the baby choir, which we were in, to the Youth Choir with the big kids. And nobody got into the Youth Choir without auditioning. In front of everyone.

Zara and Faith had already had their birthdays. Now it was up to me. We'd vowed to be ready for the next round of auditions, which were the first Thursday of the month. That meant they were a little over four weeks away, the week after my birthday. All of church's choirs would be performing in the upcoming Gospel Music Jamboree the day after Thanksgiving. And we didn't want to be stuck in the baby choir for the show.

The problem? I was still so terrified of singing in public. I was not ready.

And time was running out.

Don't miss Sherri Winston's amazing books.

STORIES ABOUT FRIENDSHIP, GROWING UP, AND FINDING YOURSELF!

Sherri Winston

is the author of *President of the Whole Fifth Grade* (a Sunshine State Young Readers Award selection); *President of the Whole Sixth Grade* (a Kids' Indie Next pick); *President of the Whole Sixth Grade: Girl Code*; *The Sweetest Sound*; *Jada Sly, Artist & Spy*; and *The Kayla Chronicles*. She lives with her family in Florida. Sherri invites you to visit her online at iamsherriwinston.com and voteforcupcakes.com.